'Suzie is back, as mad as ever. Rainbow the clumsy fairy is funny and I still love Gregor.'

(Emma, aged 9)

'This book brings alive the magic of Portland, with its stunning landscapes, rare flowers and rich history. It makes me want to visit the Isle and find out more.'

(Lisa, aged 39)

'All my favourites from The Portland Sea Dragon are here; Gregor the sheepdog, Mrs Groves and Mrs Greychurch.'

(Tem, aged 12)

'It brings old legends to life in imaginative and exciting ways.'

(Edd, aged 14)

Look out for more of

THE PORTLAND CHRONICLES

The Portland Sea Dragon

The Portland Pirates

The Island Giant

Visit www.rovingpress.co.uk

THE PORTLAND CHRONICLES

ENCHANTMENT
OF THE
BLACK DOG

CAROL HUNT

ROVING PRESS

© 2010 Carol Hunt
Published by Roving Press Ltd
4 Southover Cottages, Frampton, Dorset, DT2 9NQ, UK
Tel: +44 (0)1300 321531
www.rovingpress.co.uk

First published 2010 by Roving Press Ltd
ISBN: 978-1-906651-07-7

British Library Cataloguing in Publication Data
A catalogue record for this book is available from the British
Library

Illustrations and cover artwork by Domini Deane

Set in Minion 11.5/14 pt by www.beamreachuk.co.uk
Printed and bound by
Rzeszowskie Zaklady Graficzne S.A. Poland

Hello,

Isabel Maydew asked me to write an introduction for her story about the Black Dog of Portland. Of course, I know far more than she does about the black dog and nearly caught the animal hundreds of times. In fact, if it were not for Isabel, this would be a book about me and the black dog. Isabel is really annoying.

Anyway, the black dog is a Portland legend and an omen of bad luck. Black dogs appear out of nowhere and then vanish. Cave Hole at Portland Bill is supposed to be the lair of one of the dogs, the Roy Dog, a very frightening creature. I could tell you a lot of stuff about black dogs, but, as Isabel will show you, the real black dog of Portland turned out to be a lot more mysterious than anyone had imagined.

Miranda Greychurch
Age 14
Church Ope
Portland
Dorset

CHAPTER ONE

THE BLACK DOG AND

JELLYFISH

The first soft golden lights of dawn crept like fingers over the horizon. Isabel Maydew yawned. She was lying face down on the West Cliffs of Portland, among the wild pink thrift and yellow samphire flowers, with her eyes and nose just over the edge of the sheer plummet. Herring gulls wheeled around her, squawking at the 12-year-old girl lurking near their rocky home. Isabel waited patiently. 'Any second now,' she sighed, struggling to stay alert. Suddenly, a low wailing cry echoed across the sea, making her skin crawl. 'Urrgh!' she said, putting her fingers in her ears. As the wailing died away, she peered around, her ears still prickling. She squinted along the rocky shore.

Far below her, Isabel glimpsed a glittering tail in the inky, white-topped waves at the foot of the cliffs, then a white arm, then a swirl of coiling blood-red hair. 'The mermaid!' breathed Isabel. In the mermaid's hand was a silvery conch shell. She raised her hand and blew into the seashell. Her green eyes roamed across the sea to the sky, then to the cliffs, and fixed on Isabel. 'Oh no!' Isabel rolled out of sight and lay on her back, looking at the last flickering stars of the April night, screwing up her face

1

against the eerie noise.

As the seashell call echoed around her and faded, Isabel edged away from the cliffs, struggled to her feet and tucked her cold hands in her pockets. For a week she had been awoken by the ghostly moaning cry from the sea. This morning, she had set her alarm and sneaked out of the house at 4 o'clock to find out exactly what it was. Isabel looked around at the sky and the indigo sea, then across the windswept fields. Nothing moved. The isle of Portland was asleep. Taking a last peek over the cliffs, Isabel tried to imagine who or what the sinister mermaid was calling. Whatever it was, it wasn't going to be good. She imagined a creature with a coiled tail and a head like a giant seahorse surging from the waves.

Isabel glanced at her watch. She must get home before her sister Suzie woke up. Shivering, her coat soaked with dew, she trudged along the cliff path towards her home, a sturdy cottage overlooking West Weares. At her feet, tiny yellow and orange orchids bloomed, and across the fields coppery Portland lambs called *maaa* to their mothers. A gentle breeze tugged her hair.

Isabel jumped over a tumbledown stone wall and scrambled across a limestone rock that marked the path towards her home; one of the many chunks of rock hewn from Portland across the centuries, as valuable to the island as brandy to a smuggler. She heard a whisper of a sound, as something jumped the wall after her, padding softly along the footpath. Isabel stopped, looked round and held her breath. She heard the roar of waves against the pebbles of Chesil Beach, the cry of herring gulls, but there was something else. Something closer. Isabel froze. She saw its eyes first, green and glowing. Then there was a shadow, a black jagged outline. Finally, the creature stood in front of her, a huge dog with jet black fur, his bright eyes fixed on her. He prowled towards her. Suddenly, the mermaid blew into the shell again and the menacing black dog flinched.

'Oh, she's calling *you*!' breathed Isabel. She edged away from the dog, her back against the rock. 'I'm not afraid of you,' she added, her heart racing. The dog padded along the shadows of the bramble bushes, watching her. 'Who are you?' she whispered. The dog's eyes widened and he sank down on his haunches. Around his nose, ears and paws, traces of silvery white fur stood out against the black. He tilted his head at her. 'D'you know me?' asked Isabel, frowning. The animal stayed very still. Isabel took a deep breath and tiptoed forwards. The black dog watched her uneasily, panting, pressed to the ground, ears flattened against his head, his tail tucked low. Isabel reached out a hand towards him. She felt spiky cold fur under her fingers and the chill of icy caves ran up her arm, weighing it like stone. She pulled her hand away but leaned closer to him and gazed into his eyes, feeling a wave of deep sadness wash through her.

'You're the Black Dog of Portland!' Isabel gasped, pressing her frozen hands together. This creature was as large and menacing as a wolf, she thought, a black wolf. 'I won't hurt you,' she added quickly. The dog's eyes glistened and Isabel stretched out her hand to gently touch the dog again. Dodging her fingers, he fled, disappearing instantly.

Disappointed, Isabel rose to her feet and headed home, trying not to step on the tiny golden snails that crisscrossed her path. Lost in thought, she collided with her mother's friend Mrs Veronica Greychurch, in green wellington boots, holding a pair of huge black binoculars. Mrs Greychurch glared at her.

'What are you doing here? My daughter Miranda doesn't wander the cliffs all night like a lost sheep,' she snapped, towering over Isabel.

'Nothing. I couldn't sleep,' said Isabel, backing away from her.

Mrs Greychurch narrowed her beady eyes at Isabel. 'Well, hurry home then,' she said, without giving any explanation why she too was out at such an unusual hour of the day. As she clomped away from Isabel through the long grass, she scanned the sea with her binoculars, fixing her sights on the rocks where the mermaid lurked.

Isabel ran home through the tall golden flowers, glad to escape from creepy, annoying Mrs Greychurch. The sky around her house was still lit by a distant glimmer of stars, but the fiery lights of dawn were lighting up the east of the Isle. Isabel crossed the deserted street and pushed open the creaky garden gate. The garden was neatly mown and yellow primroses bloomed in the flower beds. The stone cottage in front of her had a sleepy air, the curtains drawn, her mother and sister still fast asleep.

Isabel shivered. Shadows seemed to cling to her, lingering at the corner of her eye like ghosts. As she walked up the garden path, she thought about the rare and strange animal she had just met, the Black Dog of Portland.

Isabel awoke from a dream about a boy cutting a flint spear from a chunk of Portland rock. She felt warm breath against her cheek. A small voice whispered in her ear, 'This is for you, it's a Happy April present!' It was Suzie, her sister.

Isabel opened one eye and heaved herself up on her elbow. In the bedroom mirror, her light brown hair stuck out on one side and lay flat on the other, like a seagull standing sideways in a Portland gale. 'Wha' time is it now?' she asked.

Suzie stared at the alarm clock. 'The big hand is on the twelve, the little hand is on the six,' she read out.

'That's 6 o'clock, Suzie. It's too early.'

Suzie put a pink box on the bed next to Isabel, her eyes glowing, her small hands shaking with excitement. She had stuck pink mermaid stickers all over the box and written *Isabell* on a small card cut into a black werewolf shape with wonky ears and sharp teeth.

Isabel sat up, her eyes drawn to the corner of the room where shadows lurked.

'What yer looking for?' asked Suzie.

Isabel shook her head, 'Nothing.'

'You're bonkers,' said Suzie, 'Open your gift, silly sausage.' She smiled from one round cheek to the other, her wavy golden hair tucked into two bunches. She was wearing her favourite pyjamas, dotted with fluffy sheep. To look at her, all pink and glowing, thought Isabel, no one would guess that Suzie, at the age of just four and three-quarters, lived a life of crime including stealing Portland sheep.

Sighing, Isabel untied the ribbons knotted around the box and looked down at a small jellyfish, floating in a puddle of water.

'He's called Figgles. You can keep him in the goldfish tank wiv Squeaky the goldfish. I love him, he's the best jellyfish ever!' shouted Suzie.

Isabel put the box down quickly, avoiding the tentacles. 'You stole it from Ocean Park yesterday, didn't you?' she said.

'Yes,' said Suzie proudly, 'and I'm going back today to have my photo taken with an octopus. They're looking for a new star for the TV show *Sea Life Special*. I'm gonna hug a shark and kiss a turtle to show everyone how caring sea creatures are, and how we have to love them and save them from getting too warm,' she explained.

'You can smuggle the jellyfish back to its tank,' said Isabel, 'Or else you'll get arrested.'

'I never get caught,' said Suzie smugly. 'Next week I'm gonna catch the fairy.'

'What fairy?' asked Isabel wearily.

'The one in the garden at *Bumbletots Nursery*, of course. I nearly got her the other day. I creeped up on her,' said Suzie. She held up the card, 'That's the doggy what came home with you when you sneaked out last night. I looked out the window. He was hiding under the bushes. He's got green eyes,' she added, making her eyes round and goggly.

Isabel shuddered and pulled the covers over her head. She could hear her mother singing as she went downstairs to start breakfast.

'I expect Ryder will be here in a minute,' said Isabel, her voice muffled.

'I hate Ryder!' snarled Suzie, her eyes narrow and menacing. 'Figgles is a gentle jellyfish, but even he wants to attack 'im.'

There was a crash downstairs that shook the house as the kitchen door flew open. 'Hey!' shouted Ryder, 'I got lost! I was sitting next door for half an hour. Ate a bit of cheese. Your neighbour shrieked her head off. Chased me out with the kitchen mop. Is there any bacon for breakfast?' Isabel looked out of her bedroom window. Mrs Hill was in the garden next door, hair in curlers, her face bright red, glaring at their kitchen door. She waved the mop at Isabel.

'He's an idiot,' hissed Suzie.

Ryder was their mother's friend. Isabel guessed he was in his early 30s. He lived in a VW camper van painted with purple flowers and loaded with a lot of surfboards. Ben Lau, her best friend, called him the Surfing Dinosaur. Ryder arrived at odd times, to fit around his surfing plans, and he was helping their mother work on a musical show in a week's time at Portland Castle. There was another crash.

'I'd better go and sort him out,' said Suzie, her mouth pinched with anger. She tucked the jellyfish box under her arm and stamped downstairs.

Isabel looked out of the bedroom window towards the gleaming blue sea. In the garden, the bluebells bobbed their heads, sparkling with dew, and seagulls soared overhead shouting *Waaark* as they prepared their nests for chicks. Near their cottage, the land dropped away in a sheer limestone cliff down to sea crashing on the rocks below. From her bedroom window, Isabel looked towards Chesil Beach, which swept in an arc of pebbles towards Moonfleet. Isabel had lived here all her life and had grown up with the Atlantic winds that shook the house and threw huge waves against the cliffs. For hundreds of years, the treacherous Portland seas had wrecked ships against Chesil, strewing treasures on the beach. For good reason the bay below Isabel's home was called Deadman's Bay.

Isabel thought about the black dog. If the mermaid *was* calling the black dog at dawn every morning, why was the animal fleeing her? Isabel had an uneasy feeling, as if the black dog had been looking for her. She knew the stories about ghostly black dogs on Portland; the black dog was a local legend, an omen of death, disaster, drowning. Isabel shivered. Yet the animal she had seen was very real. She would email her friend Ben later and find out what he knew about the dog.

Email:	**Weird Black Dog**
From:	**Isabel Maydew**
To:	**Ben Lau**
Sent:	**6 April**

Hello Ben,
D'you know anything about the Black Dog of Portland? I think I saw him earlier today on West Cliff footpath. I've put Suzie's jellyfish in the bath. She keeps trying to cuddle it, but it hasn't stung her yet. Can you set up the sound system for my mum's show with Ryder next week?
And great news! I've a new lead on the Southwell fairy!

Isabel

Email: re. Weird Black Dog

From   Ben Lau
To: Isabel Maydew
Sent: 6 April

Hi Izzie,

Thanks for your email. According to local legend, the Black Dog of Portland wanders the island at night. People claim to see him on island paths and at the caves near the lighthouse at Portland Bill. He's said to be a guardian of the underworld. In other words, he's dangerous!

I think a jellyfish would be ok in the bath for a day or two.

I'm happy to do the sound for your mother's music show with Surf Dinosaur at the Castle next week. Tell her I'll borrow some speakers and an amplifier from the school. No, I'm not looking for fairies in Southwell. There are lots of rare moths on Portland which are sometimes mistaken for fairies, I can lend you a book about them if you like.

Ben

CHAPTER TWO

STALKING THE MERMAID

Miranda Greychurch, 14 years old and a wannabe mermaid, waited at the edge of the sparkling blue sea on the east coast of Portland near Freshwater Bay, her straight blonde hair hanging over her pointed nose. She dabbed her toes in the sea. She hoped that the mermaid would come for her at last. After reading the latest vampire romances, including *Twilight*, she had decided that she really wanted to hang out with mermaids. It was easier than vampiring if you lived on the small island of Portland, plus she was scared of bats.

'Where is she?' gasped Miranda. She clasped her hands together and gazed out to sea. 'My destiny lies with mermaids beneath the waves, with the silver fish and the shipwrecks and the chests of gold.' Miranda paused to think about the mermaid's gold and the things she could buy in Weymouth with it. Like that pink miniskirt she'd seen yesterday. After all, what use was gold to a mermaid?

'Wrraff!'

Miranda jumped at the sudden bark. Gregor bounded across the pebbles to her and dropped a stone near her feet.

'Go away!' yelled Miranda, kicking the stone. Gregor raced after it. 'I can't believe I'm stuck with you again!'

Gregor was a farm dog, a scruffy collie from Groves Farm where Miranda helped out at the stables. She had been talked into walking Gregor as Mrs Groves, his owner, had a headache.

Gregor dipped his paw in the sea and looked back at Miranda. 'I'm not getting your stone for you! Find another one!' Gregor snuffled around and picked up a small pearly stone, perfectly round, that shimmered in the sun. He plopped it on Miranda's foot. Miranda sighed and picked it up. 'Yuck!' she said, tossing it into the sea.

Nearby, behind the piles of rocks that lay in cascades at the foot of the cliffs, the Portland mermaid was hiding from Miranda. She ran her marble white fingers through long, untidy red hair and pulled at the seaweed tangled around her turquoise tail. Frazzled and upset, she toyed with a large shell looped across her chest on a glittering thread.

Behind the mermaid, there was a crunch as something landed on the beach.

'Is that you, Ssouthwell fairy?' asked the mermaid, without looking round. A small figure picked herself up from the beach and dusted off a coating of sand. 'Even mothss fly better than you,' added the mermaid, with a sneer.

'Once I'm flying, it's fine,' whispered the fairy. She shook out her gauzy wings, dappled with gold and pink. 'You can't hide from Miranda forever, mermaid,' she giggled. She was tiny, no bigger than the mermaid's hand. She wore a sparkling green tunic, her hair pulled back in a white band. She jumped up and down. 'You might need to give me a lift off.'

'Be quiet, she'll hear uss,' whispered the mermaid, worriedly.

The fairy propped herself against a rock with her elbow and looked serious. 'Let me give you some advice about fans, mermaid. They pop up all the time, but they always grow out of it.' Her voice had a high ring to it, like a bell.

'Get rid of her for me, Rainbow! Miranda Greychurch is a sstalker!' hissed the mermaid. 'It'ss unnatural for a human to want to be a mermaid! We enchant the humans, draw them into the sea against their will. We strike deals, then betray them.'

Rainbow smiled behind her small hand. 'You did strike a deal! You gave gold coins to her ancestor Sally Lucke in return for a child of her flesh and blood,' she reminded the mermaid. 'So after all these years, Miranda, her very distant relative, is all yours!' she added.

The mermaid clenched her white fingers and bit her lip. She clutched the seashell. 'I don't want her, Rainbow, I want the black dog. You musst find him for me. I've called him day after day. You musst give me your word you'll find him. It will not go well for you, or any of you fairies, if you do not keep your promisses to me.' The mermaid angrily flicked salty water from her hair.

Rainbow frowned. 'The black dog,' she said thoughtfully. Not for the first time, Rainbow wondered what connected the mermaid and the spooky black hound. The black dog was an ancient animal, from the time of sea dragons and the island giant. He ran along the paths of Portland at night, crisscrossing the old fields and quarries. He was a creature of the shadows, but as much a part of the island as the lighthouse and the limestone rocks. Many times over the years, as dawn crept over the sleeping isle, Rainbow had seen the black dog run to the mermaid's side as she blew into a spiralling conch shell. Rainbow fluttered her wings nervously.

'He hass to come when I call,' insisted the mermaid. 'It'ss old magic.' The mermaid looked out to sea, towards the mists of Moonfleet, as if looking back in time. Rainbow narrowed her eyes at the mermaid. There was far more to the story of the black dog than the mermaid had ever admitted.

Gregor peered around the rock at the fairy and the mermaid. He sniffed loudly at them.

'Shooo!' said Rainbow.

Gregor retreated. He padded to Miranda and whined at her. 'Get off my foot, Gregor!'

Rainbow hopped up and down, from one toe to the other, fluttering her wings. She had made up her mind. With a little help, she could find the black dog for the mermaid. Miranda Greychurch clearly had time on her hands, but Rainbow had someone else in mind. She bounced on her toes and somersaulted into the air, flying past the mermaid's cold gleaming cheek, and finally landing on the beach again.

'Why is the black dog so important to you?' she frowned.

'That isn't your problem!' snapped the mermaid, swatting the fairy away with her hand. 'Jusst tell me when you find him.'

'I'll start my search at Groves Farm,' mused Rainbow. 'The black dog hid there once before, hundreds of years ago. D'you remember?'

'I remember!' hissed the mermaid, her emerald eyes glinting with fury. 'That sstupid girl, Sstella Groves, she took him from me. Find him, before it'ss too late.' The mermaid spun away from Rainbow with a whirl of her turquoise tail and disappeared under the sea. Gregor watched the ring of shimmering water and raised his shaggy black and white eyebrows at Miranda, who was still gazing at the far horizon, dreaming of life as a glamorous mermaid.

CHAPTER THREE

RAINBOW FINDS ISABEL

Isabel wandered along the track to Groves Farm, where her mother's cousin Mrs Groves lived, and where she also took riding lessons. It was mid-morning, Easter just 2 weeks away, the meadows rippling with long grass and tall gold and white flowers. Skylarks sang high in the vivid blue skies. Although she was nearly 13, Isabel looked forward to chocolate eggs. Last year, her little sister Suzie had eaten seven eggs in under an hour and beaten the family record.

A warm southerly wind swept across the Isle, shaking things loose and looking for mischief. It swirled into mini tornadoes, ripping washing from the lines and throwing paper from the recycling boxes into strange funnels. The retired farm horses were decked in colourful coats to protect them against the winds that always seemed to blow around Portland. Isabel wondered vaguely if Gregor, the farmhouse collie, would also be sporting a nice tartan jacket. She decided probably not, as he would have chewed a coat to bits.

A large moth flew straight into her face. Then it hung on to her nose with hands like small pincers.

'Ow!' Isabel shrieked. She blinked and sat down heavily on the haphazard stone wall that marked the ancient boundary of the Groves' farmland. She waved her hands in front of her face to get rid of the moth. A small pair of eyes swam into focus.

'Don't tell me you've never seen a Southwell fairy before!' The fairy let go of her nose and fell to the ground. Isabel leaned over to look at a small figure with wings glittering pink and gold. 'You look like a Maydew, you're not very tall and you've got fluffy brown hair. Don't you ever brush it?' commented the fairy, dusting off her dress.

'I *am* Isabel Maydew! Who are you?' asked Isabel, gobsmacked. The fairy had a small nose and slanting deep blue eyes under strong dark eyebrows.

'You can call me Rainbow,' she exclaimed.

'I've never seen a fairy,' Isabel gasped. 'My sister would love you! Can I take a photo? I've got my mobile here. My friend Ben will be amazed, he says that fairies are local folklore.'

'Most folklore is true,' snapped Rainbow. 'Forget the photo, we don't have time. I need you to look for a dog for me, a black one, looks a bit like a wolf. He's headed for Groves Farm, most likely.' She fluttered her wings, just enough to lift her from the ground and bob her up and down in the air. A gust of wind caught her and she dropped to the ground on her head.

'A dog?' said Isabel uneasily.

'Just a dog,' replied Rainbow, cheerfully upside down. There was a long silence. The fairy righted herself. 'It's a long story,' she sighed, 'The mermaid wants me to find the black dog. He's disappeared. By the way, d'you know that you look like the legendary island witch, Agnes Maydew of Weston?'

'I do know, yes,' said Isabel. Earlier in the year, she had

travelled across time and met the island witch, as well as the Portland sea dragon and smugglers. Since her time travels, life had been dull. The winter days dragged into spring, March into April. Isabel dreamt of Joseph Groves with his sword, and Sally Lucke with her gold, people who had once roamed the island but were long since forgotten by everyone except her. She wished she could travel across time again to explore the past, but with the sea dragon sleeping again, nothing seemed to happen to her. Until yesterday, when she had met the black dog. 'What *exactly* is the black dog?' she asked.

'I'm sure you must know,' said the fairy bossily. 'The black dog is an enchanted animal, a creature from old Portland, like the island giant, sea dragon and snow wolves.'

Isabel's mouth fell open. 'An enchanted dog?' she whispered, 'Who enchanted him?'

Rainbow shrugged, 'I don't know, but I know I can count on you, Isabel, to return the dog safely to the mermaid as soon as possible.'

Isabel looked across the fields towards the farm where a coil of smoke rose from the farmhouse chimney, as it had for hundreds of years. A gnarled oak tree stood between them and the old building, its branches spreading into the sky, like a hand hiding a face.

'I'm not sure about helping the mermaid,' said Isabel reluctantly, 'But you think the black dog's at Groves Farm?'

Rainbow frowned, then said, 'Yes, he may have taken this path to the farm. We call it the Giant's Footpath. It runs in a line from the windmills towards the old smugglers' steps at West Weares.'

'The Giant's Footpath! I've never seen a giant on Portland,' laughed Isabel.

'Well, thank your lucky stars,' said Rainbow. 'Let me know if you find the black dog. I'll be in Southwell, near the Old Smithy. Ask any of the children from *Bumbletots*, they know where to find me,' added Rainbow. She jumped into the air, wheeling her arms in circles and took off, flying along the straight path.

Isabel looked back at the Giant's Footpath. She smiled, thinking of a giant striding behind her. In the distance she heard a wolf howl, a chilling sound. The sun vanished behind thick clouds and suddenly it was cold, too cold for April. A white mist like smoke drifted across the south of the island, and from the haze, lines of thick ice began to zigzag across the fields towards her. Time was shifting, just like before when she'd found herself back in the Portland of olden days. Shadows ran from the trees to the south, then transformed into a pack of grey wolves running across a snowy tundra. Isabel turned to flee to the farmhouse and stopped abruptly. Her path was blocked by the black dog.

He stared at her accusingly, his fur blue-black and his eyes vivid green. Isabel stepped back to a low stone wall, her hands pressed to the cold stone. The dog bounded across the path towards her and leaped the wall easily, skimming her arm. The pack of ghostly snow wolves followed him, grey and white with golden eyes. They leaped one by one over the wall. Isabel felt the ground shift beneath her, rocking her from side to side, and the ice rushed forwards. Her feet skidded as the fields vanished under a vast slippery white wilderness. Isabel landed on her knees on the glacier, clutching the ice with her frozen fingers, as time whistled over her.

18

Miranda dropped Gregor off at Groves Farm. He had staggered into his warm bed in the kitchen, wheezing, to munch a snack of Rich Tea biscuits. As she ambled back across the field to the south of the farm, in the distance she spotted that awful Isabel Maydew. Then, luckily, Isabel seemed to have disappeared. Miranda kicked her feet through the grass. She trampled across daisies and dandelions as small white butterflies fluttered around her and bumble bees hummed busily. Miranda liked bees and tried not to tread on them. She jumped over the wall and narrowly missed a strange creature, a small gnome, wearing a hideous green dress.

'Watch out!' yelled Rainbow.

'You watch out, you evil gnome!' snarled Miranda. Rainbow froze, staring at her in horror. There was a long silence. 'Whatever …,' said Miranda. 'I don't care what you are. You're weird, so we'll leave it at that. Bye.'

Rainbow flew at her ankles, yanked at them in a judo move and Miranda fell flat on her back. 'I'm a Southwell fairy!' shouted Rainbow. 'You're a Greychurch, aren't you? Have all the islanders apart from the children at *Bumbletots* forgotten the Southwell fairies?'

'I don't think anyone nowadays wants to see fairies,' Miranda tried to struggle to her feet, but Rainbow tugged her ankles again and she flipped backwards. 'Get off my ankles!' she cried.

'I hear you want to be friends with the mermaid,' said

Rainbow, taking a different line with Miranda.

Miranda stopped struggling and listened. 'Maybe.'

'The mermaid and I go back a long way. I can talk to the mermaid if you find a certain black dog for her.'

'A black dog,' considered Miranda, her lips pursed.

'Listen,' said Rainbow, 'If you find the black dog, we can make a deal with the mermaid. The dog is a rare animal, valuable.'

Miranda sniffed. She needed to earn some money. Paper rounds were too early in the morning and babysitting was out of the question as she hated children. 'I'll give it some thought,' she said, 'After all, catching dogs is not entirely my thing.'

The fairy looked up and down the path. 'I expect the Maydew girl will get to him first anyway.'

'Isabel Maydew!' hissed Miranda, 'I can't stand her!'

The fairy folded her arms and looked pleased with herself. 'Yes, the Greychurches have always hated the Maydews. Look, just find the black dog, or you can forget your dream of sitting on a rock with the mermaid, combing your hair.'

Miranda struggled to her feet. It was true. Isabel and Miranda had been enemies for a long time, and Miranda felt that Isabel had been getting the upper hand recently. This had to stop. 'I'll find the black dog for you,' she declared. 'Isabel isn't going to beat me at this!'

CHAPTER FOUR

ISABEL MEETS

STELLA GROVES

Isabel sat up dizzily and rubbed her forehead. The icy glacier had gone. It was a light cool day, a breeze skimming the leafy oak tree beside the farmhouse. On the path in front of her was a girl of about 16, dressed in a bodice and a long skirt which fluttered around her ankles and was gathered at the front to reveal a white frilly underskirt. She had softly curling reddish-gold hair, pale eyes and large freckled arms. A black dog walked beside her. He growled at Isabel, his eyes fixed on her as if warning her to stay away.

'Be quiet, Slipknot, it's just a girl, I think.' Stella looked Isabel up and down, staring at her clothes and hair. 'Are you the girl from the travelling theatre? I heard tell it was over from Melcombe way. I'm Stella Groves from Groves Farm. I like your costume, 'specially those pantaloons,' she said, pointing at Isabel's jeans.

Isabel was too stunned to speak. Stella went on, 'I 'spect you folk need a strong horse to move your stage across the island. It's no trouble. We're pleased to have the players here. It's been 2 years since we saw a show, around Christmas, the year 1640, I think. Robert Groves, my father – Shamble we call 'im – is very happy about it. He loves the theatre.'

Stella looked curiously at Isabel. 'What name do ye come by?'

'Isabel,' she managed to splutter.

'Well, Isabel, wait here while I get my horse.'

While Stella went off to the stables, Isabel did a quick sum. 'So, this is 1642,' she breathed. She looked around, her eyes wide with excitement. Stella's black dog glared at her and dropped to its haunches. Isabel gasped. The animal was uncannily like the weird black dog she had encountered on the cliffs, with the same dark fur, silvery nose and deep golden-green eyes. The dog kept up a low, angry growl. Isabel stepped back from him. From the corner of her eye, she glimpsed the pack of snow wolves by the oak tree, resting in the shadows and watching both her and the black dog.

'Here you are, I've got Henry for you,' said Stella. She was leading a chunky brown horse with a fluffy mane. 'He's a hard worker, full of energy, a bit fiery,' said Stella, as Henry stooped to eat a tuft of grass. Stella tethered him to the gate of the field.

'Where did you find that black dog?' asked Isabel, 'I think I've seen him somewhere before.'

'You mean Slipknot?' Stella looked Isabel up and down and decided to trust her. 'I found him. I was watching for Shamble's ship near the Portland beacon. I like to see my father sail in, especially when he's been away for a while. Slipknot was in the sea, dragged by a mermaid into the cross-currents off the south of the Isle. She left him to drown and he was struggling to stay afloat. Luckily, fishermen from Wakeham had left ropes and nets by the shore and I pulled him out. He's a wild dog, he slipped the nets easy when he reached land, yet he stays at my side and I call him Slipknot, for none may keep him but me.' The black dog leaned close to Stella and she ruffled his fur. 'Mayhap the mermaid called him into the sea, a Siren call,' added Stella, 'He nearly drowned at her hands.'

'So you saved him from the mermaid?' asked Isabel, thinking of the mermaid with her seashell, calling the black dog in the 21st century.

'Yes,' said Stella, 'Even the crew on my father's ship saw the Portland mermaid dragging a black dog out to sea. They fear the Sirens, they say they're bad luck for sailors.'

'Not too good for black dogs either,' said Isabel wryly.

Stella frowned at her, 'Anyway, he's been with me ever since. I gave him a bath in my father's tub and he scrubbed up nicely.' Stella stroked the dog's fur. 'He's mine now. I won't share him with anyone. I don't let him near the sea where the mermaid lurks.'

'I'm sure he's safer here at the farm, for now,' said Isabel.

Stella shook her head, 'You may say that, but someone tried to steal him just this morning. A man broke into the farmhouse, he smashed a cup and ate most of the bread and cheese. He tried to put a leash on Slipknot. He spoke strangely – it sounded like 'chill out dood', whatever that means. I chased him off. Slipknot must be a rare creature. Why do *you* ask about him?'

'I just wondered,' said Isabel.

Stella looked at her coldly. 'No one is taking Slipknot from me. No demon and no witch!' Stella leaned forward until her snubbed freckly nose was close to Isabel's. 'No one,' she warned.

Isabel backed away from her, glimpsing a familiar

salmon-pink t-shirt disappearing through the trees near the farmhouse, worn by a man chomping his way through a loaf of bread. 'Ryder?' she said, puzzled.

'It's him again!' shrieked Stella, 'I'll fetch the sword from the attic!' Isabel stared after Ryder as Stella dashed into the farmhouse. It was 1642. What was Ryder doing here and why would he be looking for the black dog in any case?

Isabel broke into a run after Ryder. She darted around the oak tree, the wolves leaping after her, and headed west along the Giant's Footpath. Isabel felt the wolves at her heels as the ground blurred and the fields vanished. The pack of snow wolves ran with her into a wilderness of muddy snow, a melting glacier under a stony grey sky. The wolves carried her forward, faster and faster across time. Flakes of snow blew into her face, stinging her skin, and the wind whipped against her.

Exhausted, Isabel staggered to her knees in the snow and the wolves parted like a river and surged around her. Their paws threw up a spray of melting ice water. Isabel reached out her hand and touched something smooth and metallic. Brushing the snow from her eyelashes, Isabel saw the silver-grey of a street lamp. She clutched the familiar post, gasping with relief. As the snow melted around her and poured into the drains, Isabel stood up and stamped her soaking feet on the pavement. Wet paw prints led away from her along Weston Street. The wolves had gone. She was back in her own time. In the distance, Ryder ambled up the road, still eating the bread, flakes of snow thawing in his hair.

'Hey!' shouted Isabel. Ryder climbed into his camper van, parked at the side of the road, and chugged off in a cloud of exhaust fumes. Her hands shaking, Isabel dusted snow and ice from her shirt. She had a lot of questions for Ryder. The surfer clearly wanted to get his hands on the black dog, yet she had never seen Ryder do anything except eat, surf and play the guitar. Isabel wondered how he had become mixed up with the elusive black hound. She sighed. With a mermaid and a surfer on his tail, the black dog seemed to be in a lot of trouble.

CHAPTER FIVE

FRIENDS OF DRAGONS

The Portland Friends of Dragons
Welcome New Members!

Come and meet us at White Stones Cafe.
Share a chocolate biscuit and discuss your views on
dragons. Buy a special dragon t-shirt.

Further details from Mrs Veronica Greychurch
Telephone 01305 111333

After *The Friends* meeting, Mrs Greychurch, Miranda's mother, sat in the kitchen of Mrs Groves' old family farmhouse which dated back to the 1500s. The two women were great friends and their friendship had stood a number of tests, the most recent being Mrs Groves' secret sea dragon, which Mrs Greychurch had wanted to kill. After changing her mind about dragons, Mrs Greychurch had set up *The Portland Friends of Dragons*, placing adverts in Easton Library and *The Free Portland News* for new members.

Mrs Greychurch had also recently taken up dating.

'We were meant to go out for dinner at The Heights. I

booked a lovely table with a view across the Bay. He was late!' Mrs Greychurch blew her nose angrily with a honking sound. Gregor jumped up and plonked his paws in her lap, panting hot dog breath in her face. He was overexcited after being shut in the farmhouse while Mrs Groves attended the *Dragons* meeting. 'I'm as gentle as a dove, all my friends know that, but even I couldn't stand for this,' added Mrs Greychurch.

'Mmm,' said Mrs Groves.

'So I nipped round to his house and hit him across the ears with a firm cushion (not my best one). "How dare you be late!" I declared. My lovely cushion was scuffed. I've scrubbed it with Vanish but there's still a mark.' Mrs Greychurch seized a cushion from a kitchen chair. 'Shall I show you how I hit him?'

'No!' said Mrs Groves hurriedly, 'You'll frighten Gregor.'

Mrs Greychurch blew her nose again. Gregor leaped away with a startled bark. Her normally tidy white hair had escaped its clips.

'Still,' said Mrs Groves, 'He was better than the car salesman you met on *Lovelyfellas.com*, the one who tried to sell you a Mini. He also didn't ask for money, unlike you know, the other one with the boat ....'

'You mean Neville,' said Mrs Greychurch, 'I met him on *Twitter*.'

'Yes, he borrowed money and never paid it back, twit or not,' said Mrs Groves, a little snappily. Mrs Groves could not see the point in dating. After all, she and Gregor, her beloved collie, were happy with one another. However, the winter had been long and dark. Even the coming of spring and the brighter days had not lifted Mrs Groves' spirits this year. In the evenings, low dark shadows like wolves slithered along the stable walls, and Mrs Groves had been nervous of working with the horses at dusk. So she had been thrilled when her 16-year-old nephew had turned up on the doorstep to stay with her a week ago.

Luckily, Mrs Greychurch seemed to have forgotten that she was annoyed. She jumped up to make some tea. 'I hear your nephew is staying here,' she called over her shoulder. 'It's nice for you to have company at the farm.'

'Yes, he's a quiet lad, no trouble, out most of the time. I hardly know he's here. Doesn't say much. Fond of cake, mind you. Gregor's a little upset with him.'

Gregor eyed the two of them from the rug. He was mystified that the strange boy was allowed treats whenever he wished, while he, Gregor, was given only the odd biscuit. Mrs Groves had even been making cakes for the boy, rich fruit cakes, which Gregor was also not allowed. There was something about the boy he didn't like. He didn't smell right.

'Gregor's jealous,' added Mrs Groves. Gregor flattened his ears to his head. 'He's not used to sharing me with anyone.'

'What's your nephew's name?' asked Mrs Greychurch.

'Funny thing, that,' said Mrs Groves, flushing pink across the cheeks. 'It's on the tip of my tongue, but I cannot for the life of me remember. I keep guessing, but nothing sounds quite right. He's the son of a distant cousin, a Groves. I haven't the heart to ask him to remind me of his name. It's a bit embarrassing. After all, I am his aunt.'

'Very awkward,' agreed Mrs Greychurch, on her feet by the kitchen cupboards, clanking cups. 'I expect it'll come back to you.'

Mrs Greychurch balanced a teetering pile of biscuits on a plate. She was a tall, handsome woman, thought Mrs Groves, although she wore far too much orange lipstick. Mrs Groves did not approve of make-up. She never wore any herself, dressed in the same style trousers and knitted jumper every day, with her wispy, fair hair straggling around her face.

Gregor's eyebrows wiggled as he watched Mrs Greychurch and the plate of biscuits.

'Here you are, good boy, a lovely biscuit,' she said. 'One sugar or two?' Gregor slunk off to his warm bed by the oven, crunching.

'Two sugars,' said Mrs Groves. She busied herself stuffing a knitted tea-cosy over the teapot. While Gregor was distracted by Mrs Greychurch and the biscuits, Mrs Groves sneaked out of the kitchen door. She plopped an extra bowl of dry dog biscuits out of sight around the corner of the barn. She had been feeding a wild black dog for months. Mrs Groves looked south across the fields. There he was, a black shadow moving through the trees. He would not come close if she remained. Reluctantly, Mrs Groves left the food for him.

As she walked back to the farmhouse, she remembered the long, hot summers when she had roamed the Portland fields as a young girl, walking as far south as Culverwell and dreaming of having her own beautiful black dog by her side. She collided with Gregor, who greeted her in the kitchen with crumbs stuck to his nose. 'Hmm,' she said. In many ways, life had not turned out as she had expected.

Mrs Groves peered through the kitchen window at the small statue of the mermaid at the side of the pond. She must replace the statue, it was so badly chipped. A piece of the arm was missing. The mermaid held something in her hand, but the stone was broken. Was it a seashell? She couldn't remember. She had chosen it because the mermaid had a large dog carved by her side. It was an unusual statue. Mermaids and dogs did not normally go together. Gregor knocked it over regularly with his tail. But she still quite liked it. The rain drizzled down, dripping off the mermaid's cheeks and shadows flickered around the statue. Her imaginary wolves were back. Mrs Groves closed the curtains firmly to keep out the night.

Ryder was seated at the kitchen table when Isabel arrived home from the *Friends* meeting. She put her new *Dragon* t-shirt over the back of a kitchen chair and glared at him. He smelled of sea salt and the fish paste sandwiches that he was munching. He had unloaded his van, dumping a dripping surfboard across the kitchen floor and propping his guitar by the table. Wet socks and a wetsuit lay in a damp pile under the table. A tall boy of about 16 sat next to him, with long arms and legs and dark brown hair curling around his neck. His skin was dark as if he spent long days outdoors.

'Hey, this is Izzie, the one and only. I was just talking about my board. It's a *Kangaroo* surfboard. Really it's a scaled down longboard with trim and glide features, a quad fin custom model. The surf was huge this morning at the Bill. I crashed into the shore at this kind of weird angle, hurt my leg, right here around the knee.'

'Oh,' said Isabel, thinking about seeing Ryder at the farm. 'Where did you go yesterday, Ryder?'

'Met this young guy earlier, Izzie,' Ryder said, ignoring the question. 'He's staying at Groves Farm. Can't leave the *Kangaroo* board outside on the car – 'fraid it might get scratched. It's pretty beat up already. Bad news, my best board was taken. Gotta get it back. That mermaid dude was really stroppy about my surfboard. She said I surfed over her tail. She won't give it back till I find her black dog. I spotted him on the track to Groves Farm, but then I lost him. There's a weird girl staying at the farm, d'you know her? Red hair, big dress, very emotional, yelled at me,' said Ryder, picking up another sandwich. 'Anyway, I've brought my guitar. I'm going to write a song called *Me, the surf and the lost dog, give me back my board, fishy babe*,' he waffled. He leaned over his guitar, strumming, with the sandwich between his teeth.

'Ryder,' interrupted Isabel, 'You say a mermaid took your board?'

'Gorgeous girl with a tail took it, sharp teeth,' said Ryder, running his fingers through wildly windswept hair. 'But don't worry, I'll get the dog back for the fishy chick, no hassles.'

'But you said you saw a *mermaid*? Don't you think that's strange?'

Ryder chewed the sandwich, looking at her blankly. 'Naah, surfers like me see all kinds of fish.'

Isabel sighed. 'D'you know where she is now?'

Ryder shrugged, 'Nope.'

Isabel turned to the boy, 'Did *you* see the mermaid?'

He shook his head and pushed his dark hair back from his eyes. Isabel frowned thoughtfully. The boy's face was strong and determined, with straight dark brows. She tried not to stare at him. He looked out of place in the kitchen and also strangely familiar, as if she had met him somewhere before.

Suzie stood in the kitchen doorway, staring at the back of Ryder's head with her hands on her hips. She was wearing a blue t-shirt with *Surfer* on it, but had changed it with a black marker pen to read *I hate Surfers, they Stinck*.

Their mother rushed past them looking pink, clutching sheets of music and lyrics. 'What's that man doing here again?' Suzie demanded loudly, pointing at Ryder.

'Ryder and his new friend are joining us. Won't that be great? We're going to practise a couple of songs. Ryder will be doing music later for the show. We can all sing together, with his guitar,' said Mrs Maydew.

Suzie walked into the kitchen, propped her elbows on the kitchen table and stared at Ryder. He slurped his mug of tea and cast his eye over the *Dorset Echo*, looking for the weather reports. The telephone rang.

Ryder jumped, dropping his mug, which smashed into several pieces.

'Clumsy!' shouted Suzie.

'Never mind,' said Mrs Maydew, 'We've plenty more mugs.' She picked up the phone and took it into the lounge. The boy turned to look at Isabel with clear, green eyes. He smiled suddenly, his eyes crinkling at the corners, as if she were an old friend.

'We haven't got plenty of mugs,' said Suzie, 'He broke two last week.'

Ryder read from the *Echo*. 'Force 5 tomorrow. Punchy wind. Bet it's a north-easterly. No good for windsurfing. Waves'll be too choppy.'

Mrs Maydew returned to the kitchen and mopped the floor.

'Can I call the police? I can't find my jellyfish. It's a missing item,' said Suzie.

'Ryder took it back to Ocean Park this morning. You can't keep a jellyfish in the bath,' said Mrs Maydew.

'Ryder took it!' cried Suzie, slowly, an evil glint in her eye.

Trying to ignore the look, her mother continued hastily, 'That was Mrs Groves on the phone. She's calling back in a mo. Gregor was sick on her foot. He's been in the cake tin.'

The telephone rang again and Mrs Maydew dashed to answer it. 'Hello? Oh dear, has he? Perhaps you should put him outside? Yes, I know he always rolls in the mud. Yes, that would make things worse.'

The back door crashed open. Ben, Isabel's best friend, came in with an electric guitar strapped to his back. He was lugging a large red amplifier. Isabel ran to help him with the amp.

'I see the Surf Dinosaur's here yet again,' he whispered, looking at Ryder. He looked around the room. 'D'you know who that is?' he hissed, nodding his head towards the dark-haired boy. 'Is it him, the guitarist from *Solar Enemy*? He's a real star!'

Ben fussed at his black fringe until it hung straight down over one eye, then set up his amp in the middle of the kitchen, plugged in the guitar and cranked it up loud.

'This is the guitar solo from the latest *Muse* track, I'm going to add some reverb,' he announced, trying to catch the boy's eye.

'Yeah, when's dinner?' shouted Ryder over the noise, 'I'm in a bit of a hurry. Things to do. There's a missing dog.'

'That was Groves Farm again on the phone!' shouted Mrs Maydew at the boy. 'Mrs Groves wants to know if you're coming home for dinner. Can you walk Gregor when you get back as she's tired? Can you tell her exactly what time you plan to be back? And can you bring some eggs? She'd like you to hurry up as Gregor's anxious to go out for a walk as soon as possible. He's eaten all the fruit cake and still doesn't feel well. I think that was all. Here, take the phone. She wants to tell you herself.'

CHAPTER SIX

THE SHADOW OF WAR

At her neat house on the road winding past Portland Museum to Rufus Castle, Mrs Greychurch floated downstairs in her lilac dressing gown. She smiled with delight when she saw the box in her porch. Her delivery had arrived. She dragged the box into her lounge and carefully unwrapped the large parcel. There was layer after layer of brown paper.

'Must be careful,' she whispered to herself, brushing her hair out of her eyes. 'Oh yes, my dear, that mermaid won't know what's hit it, the filthy creature.' Mrs Greychurch sat back on the cushions of her comfortable sofa and looked down at the harpoon stretched across her lap. The tip of the spear gleamed with horrible sharpness, surrounded by spikes that would render the mermaid helpless. Mrs Greychurch touched her finger to the point. The spearhead was the sharpest thing she had ever touched, made of silvery metal, the end attached to a thin rope to haul it back.

'Ouch,' she said, her eyes glowing with hatred. 'Perfect!' She had ordered the harpoon off the internet from *Youandyourhandyharpoon.com*. She rummaged in the box, finding the pivot and the launcher, a small cannon to fire the harpoon. It was so beautiful she felt tears spring to her eyes. She stroked the cannon.

Mrs Greychurch had first spotted the mermaid at Church Ope Cove last week, perched on a rock early in the morning, gazing around as if she had lost something and blowing a racket on some dreadful shell. At first, she thought it was a lovely seal, but then realised with horror that it was a mermaid, a nasty dangerous creature.

Growing up at Church Ope, a place haunted by stories of local mermaids, Mrs Greychurch had always had a deep loathing of the creatures. She especially hated the idea of their cold Siren beauty, tempting passers-by into the sea. She had scoured the coast of Portland ever since, and had finally found the mermaid lurking by West Weares. Luckily, that dozy girl Isabel had not noticed the mermaid.

'It's my job to kill the fishy thing, get rid of it before it does any harm, dragging some poor child into the sea.' She was thinking of her own daughter, Miranda, who seemed to have developed an unhealthy obsession with mermaids, which her mother was understandably keen to stamp out. The harpoon would offer her a nice, clean shot from a safe distance.

She slipped on a long pair of black gloves. 'Of course, no one must know it's me, an Avenging Angel. I'll work undercover,' she said to herself, placing the harpoon on its pivot and setting it up to fire.

She pictured the evil mermaid in front of her. She clutched the harpoon, swivelled it wildly and fired. There was an explosion of cushions and fluff as the chair by the fireplace blew up and littered the room with fabric, tumbling like confetti. Mrs Greychurch sat back. The harpoon was excellent, just the job. 'Hah!' she said. 'This will be easy!'

Stella Groves set a fire in the hearth and swept the floor of the kitchen. It was one of the first fine spring days they had seen in 1642, but the Portland wind kept a chill in the air, shaking the new green leaves on the oak tree. Despite the size of the farmhouse, there was not much to do indoors. She and Shamble, her father, rarely used any of the downstairs rooms apart from the kitchen and the dining room. Stella kept the mahogany dining table polished with beeswax, as important local men from the Court Leet sometimes met there quietly, to manage the affairs of the Isle. The farm had been built by her family and was a long building, just one room deep. Upstairs were bedrooms and a couple of empty rooms. Narrow stairs led up to the attic in the roof.

Stella took the broom from beside the back door and headed over to the stables, the buildings there in better shape than the farmhouse, whitewashed and spruce. Horses peered over their stable doors at her. Her father was fond of horses, like his older brother Joseph, who had sailed for the Americas 6 years ago in 1636, leaving the farm to be run by Stella and her father. From time to time he sent them shipments of brandy and tobacco, neither of which Stella found very useful. As Shamble was also often away fighting the French and Spanish, Richard Lucke, from a small cottage on Weston Street, now managed the farm for them. Richard was a nephew of the mysterious Sally Lucke who had vanished from the Isle many years ago amidst stories of a sea dragon and stolen gold. Richard's father, Jacob Lucke, was a hard-working quarryman who had won respect for the Lucke family name, and Richard himself was a quiet, honest man. He had worked the Groves fields since he was a young lad. The farm was doing well, making a profit from the wool of the robust Portland sheep.

Richard was at the stables, with a pocketful of last autumn's apples from the farm orchard for the horses. He smiled at Stella.

'It's a fine day,' he said cheerfully. 'I can handle the horses if you've other work to do.'

Stella smiled shyly at him, 'Shamble's home again and we've some good mackerel for dinner. The White lads from Southwell caught 'em just this morning. You can drop by and eat with us.'

Richard took off his hat, his golden-brown hair tousled around his ears. 'You know your father doesn't like me, Stella, he'll have the muskets out.' Stella blushed pink, her cheeks aglow. 'Wonder how long he'll stay with war coming,' continued Richard. 'I'd brave them guns of his to ask for your hand. He has a poor view of me, but he'd agree to the match at once if I were a soldier or a smuggler. What's this dog you have here?' he added, looking at Slipknot. 'Never seen a black dog like him before. Not much of a farm animal. Wild, I'd say, like a wolf.'

'No, no, wolves are grey. I think Slipknot's a rare dog. I caught him in the sea. Yet a stranger came to the farm yesterday, looking for him.'

'Did he bother you?' asked Richard.

'No, but he smelled strange, like sea salt and crab soup. He tried to catch Slipknot. He wore an odd pair of blue pantaloons that ended by his knees. When I enquired what he wanted, he asked for an apple for pudding as he'd been "wind zurfing". Whoever heard of such strange things? I chased him out. Then I saw that all the bread, two apples, a pat of butter and half a pot of jam had gone. A strange robber for sure.'

'I never heard of demons with such a hearty appetite!' said Richard, 'Yet it would be better if you weren't always alone, Stella.'

'I can look after myself,' she insisted.

'You know what I mean,' said Richard. 'You shouldn't have to fear strangers, nor keep a black wolf by your side.'

'Father won't speak of my future.'

'No, it suits him to keep matters just as they are,' said Richard, 'You take care of everything for him.'

Stella stooped to clench her fingers in the dog's thick black fur. 'Civil War's coming to the island, Richard. Who knows what may happen? Look at the rest of Dorset, where brother turns against brother and families are divided in faith. We cannot speak of anything else at this fearful time.'

Richard looked downcast. The dog gazed up at him, as if he understood what Richard was thinking. Richard shivered. It was no ordinary animal, but fearsome enough to protect Stella as the shadow of war crept closer to the Isle.

CHAPTER SEVEN

AT OCEAN PARK

Isabel and Ben trailed around Ocean Park in an April shower, following Suzie who was wearing a shiny blue and green octopus costume with dangling tentacles. A camera crew tracked Suzie, hanging on her every word, zooming in for close-ups of her face. Isabel and Ben walked behind her, trying to stay out of range of the camera.

'These are crabs,' announced Suzie, 'They're very friendly and make good pets.' She picked up a dripping wet spider crab and tried to kiss the shell, but the crab fixed its claw on her nose. Suzie waited patiently while Isabel stepped forward and prised her loose.

'We've been here all day. They must have enough film for this week's show by now,' Isabel whispered.

Suzie glared at her from inside her sparkly costume. 'Now I'll lead the way to the stingray tank to show you how to hold a ray by the tail. They love it,' Suzie shouted.

Suzie and the camera crew hurried off. Isabel sank on to a rock beside the crab pool and sighed. Ben patted her shoulder with a fin. He was dressed as a shark for Suzie's piece on gentle basking sharks, and could only just move his hand. He looked at Isabel through a jaw lined with jagged teeth. After filming, he had painted dripping blood around the teeth. A toddler waddled past them and shrieked. The mother looked crossly at him.

'Ben, d'you believe in fairies?' asked Isabel.

Ben looked at her from the shark's mouth, 'No, I believe in moths and local folklore. Now I'm going to get some lunch. Want anything?' Isabel shook her head. Ben waddled off to the cafe.

Isabel leaned over the crab pool, tracing her fingers in the shallow water. She had to track down the mermaid and find out why she was calling the black dog. Was she planning to kill the animal? Isabel watched the swirly patterns in the pool, the light sparkling on the water like tiny stars.

'Hello Izzie,' shouted Ryder from a swingboat above her.

'Ryder?' said Isabel, gazing up at the swingboat.

'Amazing ...!' yelled Ryder as he swung by.

'I don't think you're meant to go that high,' called Isabel.

'What a rush, dude!' he shouted, scrabbling to his feet and standing with one foot on the seat at the front, riding it like a surfboard.

A red-faced man in an Ocean Park shirt hurried towards the swings.

'Hey you!' he yelled. 'I've got enough problems with the shark!'

'I 'spect you know me!' shouted Ryder as he zipped past, 'Won the local Windsurfing Champs in 1999. I don't mind if you take photos!' The swingboat soared into the sky, the chains straining.

The man looked at Isabel. 'I don't know him,' she said, sliding away. She edged through the growing crowds around the swingboats and headed for the exit. A furious Suzie was bustling towards the boats with the camera crew. Suzie would sort out Ryder. Isabel wanted to find the elusive mermaid.

The mermaid sat on a rock near the curving bay of Church Ope Cove, feeling the light touch of spring rain on her cold skin. She tilted her face up to the watery afternoon sun and closed her eyes. Her back ached. She drummed her fingers on the rock. The black dog was slipping away from her, she could sense it. She could smell the change in the air. The enchantment was fading. He was lingering in the company of humans, out of her reach.

The mermaid shuddered. What would happen if the black dog remembered? She ground her sharp teeth and glared at the sandy cliffs that meandered along the coast to the Grove. She toyed with a strand of seaweed, pulling it to shreds. She needed that stupid surfer or the fairy to bring her the black dog. Surely one of them would be able to find him before it was too late? She gazed towards the southern horizon where the lost islands of Atlantis, her old home, had long since vanished beneath the sea. She drummed her fingers again.

On the shore a small figure ran down the winding steps to the Cove. The mermaid hissed as the girl stopped and stared at her, 'Issabel Maydew!' The girl asked too many questions, and she had set the sea dragon free.

'Wait, mermaid!' called Isabel, but the mermaid flexed her powerful turquoise tail and disappeared into the sea.

CHAPTER EIGHT

TRAINING GREGOR

'Gregor, fetch!' commanded Mrs Groves. She was wearing large leather gloves and a brown hat with a feather in the brim. They had been out in the field by the farmhouse for over an hour, working on Gregor's training. Gregor looked at the bouncy ring that had landed with a plop in the field. Isaac the horse edged closer to get a better view over the fence from the next field. A gusty west wind whistled around them. Mrs Groves had made her mind up. Spring was here and she had always longed for Gregor to compete in dog agility.

'Fetch it!' shouted Mrs Groves. She sighed and went to pick up the ring. Gregor pounced and snatched the toy from her hand, bounding away across the field. At a safe distance, he stopped with the ring gripped between his teeth.

'I'm not chasing you. Come here and I'll throw it for you!'

Gregor danced away, keeping one eye on Mrs Groves, his fluffy black ears pointed, his tail waving. He dropped the ring, backed away from it and looked at Mrs Groves. Isaac whinnied.

'I know, Isaac, he's hopeless. OK, Gregor, let's tackle the obstacle course.' Mrs Groves led him to the course. She had piled up some baked bean tins and put planks over them for Gregor to run across, and further along the field she had made three low horse jumps for him to leap over. She had also bought a canvas tunnel from the hardware shop in Easton. Mrs Groves and Gregor faced each other at the start of the course, Gregor panting with excitement.

'Now, watch me, Gregor. You jump over here, run across here, then you go through the tunnel ....' Gregor watched with interest as Mrs Groves crawled along the canvas tunnel. He pounced on the tunnel and bit it, squashing it flat, growling and ripping the fabric. He leaped up with Mrs Groves' hat between his teeth. 'No, leave it. Gerroff!' said a muffled voice.

Finally, Mrs Groves struggled out of the tunnel and leaped over the horse jump. Gregor bounced from side to side, barking with excitement and set off around the edge of the field in a wild run with the hat. 'Stop, you silly dog!' bawled Mrs Groves.

Gregor flew around the field, his tail trailing like a streamer. His legs thundered beneath him, pounding the ground. He went faster around a curve near the gate, narrowly missing the fence where Isaac leaned, and shot into the straight run like a black and white rocket. Mrs Groves watched him with her hands on her hips. She shivered, 'Ooh, it's chilly.'

Frowning, she looked towards the hedgerows. The wild black dog watched her from the shadows, his fur so black it gleamed in the sunlight. He gazed back at her with round green eyes. Mrs Groves felt an icy chill running down her back. 'Oh dear, Gregor won't like him at all.'

Gregor was making another lap, his paws hardly touching

the ground. He saw the black dog as he roared past Mrs Groves. Tripping over his paws, he rolled like a black and white cannonball across the field and landed in a ditch.

'Gregor!' shrieked Mrs Groves, 'I wish you'd slow down!' She glanced over her shoulder, relieved to find the black dog had vanished.

Her nephew was striding across the field towards them. Mrs Groves noted that his dark hair fell almost to his shoulders. She would have to take him for a hair-cut at the barbers in Easton, smarten him up. Gregor staggered out of the ditch with grass matted in his fur and sniffed at the boy. He smelled of wood smoke and old dark places. Gregor's hackles rose.

'We've been training. Gregor did quite well,' said Mrs Groves. 'Stop sniffing, Gregor. We'll have to try again tomorrow. Come on, let's get you a biscuit.' She was annoyed with herself for being startled by the wild black dog. She would put more food out for him later when no one was around. She was worried about him. The dog must be lonely, roaming the fields on his own. She wished she could help him more. She would offer him a home, if only that were possible.

CHAPTER NINE

STELLA AND CIVIL WAR

Isabel walked past the old windmills that stood at Cottonfields and Top Growlands. The mills reminded Isabel of two old soldiers, standing guard over the south of the Isle. After glimpsing the mermaid at Church Ope yesterday, she had searched the east coast again from The Grove, through Cheyne Weares and all the way down to Freshwater Bay, and was wondering where to look next. Isabel shoved her hands in her jeans pockets and scuffed her feet. She remembered the mermaid's sinister hissing voice and coiling red hair. In January, she had attacked Isabel and nearly drowned her. Isabel gazed south across the quarries and fields where the legendary black dog roamed, to the sea churning over the Portland Race, where powerful sea currents frothed and clashed. There, the mermaid had tried to drown the black dog in 1642. Isabel remembered her strong white fingers, as cold and hard as marble.

'I need to speak to her, she knows the real story of the black dog,' thought Isabel. Suddenly, despite the spring sunshine, she felt icy cold. She gasped. The shadowy pack of wolves was running from the south, panting as if they had crossed a vast terrain to reach her. Isabel stood very still as the wolves surrounded her. No longer ghostly, their fur was soft grey and white and their shining yellow eyes were outlined with black, making their stare deep and piercing. The pack rested, some lying on their sides, the larger wolves watching her warily and licking their paws as if they dared her to run away. Two of the younger cubs rolled and tumbled on the ground, play fighting. Isabel smiled as they rolled round and round, batting each other with paws that seemed too big for their small legs.

One smaller cub ran to her and tugged at her jeans with his small teeth. Isabel leaned over and rubbed his white fluffy stomach as he rolled playfully at her feet. The cub bounced around her, yipping. Isabel laughed.

The large upright wolf with the snowy ruff across his chest approached her, his tail held straight behind him. He gently gripped her jeans with his teeth and tugged. 'Ok, I understand, you want me to come with you,' said Isabel nervously. The wolf released her and, glancing back at her just once, walked off towards the windmills. As she followed, a gentle flurry of snow brushed her face and for a split second she saw the blinding white of the ancient island glacier as she stepped out of her own time and into another century.

A musket shot whistled overhead from a clump of trees. Isabel clasped her hands over her head and hid behind a windmill. A group of men in deep-red coats carrying long pikes ran across the edge of a clearing in front of her and disappeared into the trees.

'He's carrying the letter!'

There was more gunshot and smoke left blue-grey trails in the air.

'He's come up by St Andrew's Church!' a soldier shouted.

Isabel ran low to the ground with her hands over her ringing ears. She darted from tree to tree and ducked behind a large bramble. Suddenly it was quiet. The wind whispered across the branches. Isabel listened. She had a horrible feeling there was something behind her. She turned around slowly. Stella Groves was crouching behind a holly bush with a man lying injured beside her.

'Come and help me, Isabel!' Stella cried. 'Father's taken a shot to the arm.'

Isabel ran to her side and looked down at the injured man. He was wearing dark breeches, greyish stockings and large brown boots, coated in mud.

'Let's prop him up against a tree,' suggested Isabel. They grabbed him under each arm of his shabby brown doublet coat and hauled him up against a slender birch tree.

Shamble opened one eye. 'Got the letter. Portland Castle will stand for the King!' he rasped, shaking his fist after the soldiers. '*A brave man, he fought high and low, No one knew where he would go ...,*' Shamble sang, his eyes closed happily as Stella peered at the wound on his arm.

'Just a nick, by the looks of it. A fisher boat made it to the cove from Melcombe and brought this letter for the Rector of St Andrew's. As he's still sick with fever, he called upon Shamble to take it. Shamble was lucky to escape the soldiers from Dorchester who tailed him.'

'They're afeared the good King will make for Portland Castle and none may touch him there, not with all them cannons!' said Shamble, tapping the side of his nose. 'Gave them the slip easy. Us Groves men are slippery on our own soil. A drop of brandy wouldn't go amiss, young maid, for the wound. If I'd got closer to them wi' me sword, I'd have skewered the lot of 'em!'

'Let's get you back to the farm,' said Stella, 'You don't need brandy.'

'You've hidden the brandy again, hav' you!' roared Shamble.

'It's not hidden, it's in the larder,' argued Stella, her cheeks flushed.

'Your ole Uncle Joseph wouldn't stand for that!'

'Richard Lucke doesn't drink at all,' snapped Stella.

'Has that boy been a-courtin' again? I'll not have it! You don't need to wed a Lucke. You'll have the farm when I'm gone.'

'You're not here very often *now*. Richard runs the farm for us.'

'The farm is *my* home and castle till they bury me 'neath the ground, young maid! You'll not marry that lad! Why, he takes no interest in war and grand matters. I've not seen him even handle a sword. The Lucke family are good for Slingers and nothing more. Hear him talk, with his wheat, barley and oats.'

'He knows the land well, the Portland soil is hard but he grows crops for us year on year. The men work hard for him. The quarries offer better pay than farm work, but John Attwooll and William Stone stay to work for Richard – he's a fair man.'

'I'll skim his tail with musket shot if I hear more of 'im!'

They tottered from the trees and across the meadow towards the farmhouse, with Shamble and Stella arguing loudly about Richard Lucke and the brandy. A single skylark sang over them, a long chirrupy song. A sea mist rolled down the island from The Heights and a light drizzle covered them.

'True Portland weather, these sea mists hide us in the clouds,' remarked Shamble. 'Have you still got that evil black dog in the kitchen? It's a bad omen.'

'Slipknot is harmless. He's afeared o' you.'

'I'll fear him with my best boot if he comes near me,' sniffed Shamble.

Stella helped Shamble into a chair in the kitchen and lifted the brandy and a small glass down from the top cupboard. Shamble took the bottle firmly from her and swigged from it. Isabel noticed a vase of bluebells on the kitchen window. Stella followed her gaze.

'Shamble always brings me bluebells,' smiled Stella, 'They're my favourite flower.'

Isabel sat down on a wooden stool by the kitchen table and looked around with interest. The kitchen was paved with grey stone slabs and a wooden dresser held all the plates, stacked neatly. Gregor would have knocked over the plates in the 21st century farmhouse, thought Isabel. Yet it felt the same, homely and friendly. There were herbs hanging from the beams and a big cool larder to the side of the kitchen where Isabel glimpsed baskets stacked with russet apples. The black dog watched her with unblinking green eyes from the corner of the room.

'You one of them actors from away?' asked Shamble, looking a lot happier with the bottle in his hand. Stella mixed a poultice near the window, returning to daub it on Shamble's arm.

'I guess so,' said Isabel.

'Not up with the latest news, I 'spect, of men fightin' their own kinfolk and turnin' our country upside down with

Civil War?' asked Shamble.

'I guess not,' said Isabel.

'High time young maids like you and Stella understood what we're fightin' for. I help the Court Leet who govern the island for the Lord of the Manor, the King himself,' said Shamble, sweeping a clear space on the kitchen table. A silver dish holding a pat of butter teetered on the edge of the table. Stella hurled herself forward and caught it. Shamble loaded objects on to the table.

'Give me that flagon,' he said, 'and the candlesticks. The forks over here, they're the Puritans. Now if we put the fire shovel and tongs here, that'll show 'em a thing or two.'

'We have two armies,' he announced, lining up the small silver pots of salt and pepper against the round cob of bread. 'We have the Royalists, who follow good King Charles. We're in the Royal Manor here, my girl! This other lot are the forces of Parliament, and a serious lot they are! Puritans, we call 'em! They won't have dancing nor even a drop of brandy. They ain't keen on Charlie, God bless the King – say he's a spendthrift. Folk don't like that, not one bit, but he's still our King.'

Shamble pushed a pot of honey, a blue and white jug of milk and various bowls and plates around the table, with the King on one side and the forces of Parliament on the other.

'So, Dorchester is with Parliament now?' asked Isabel, 'That's only an hour away from us.'

Shamble glowered at her under his bushy eyebrows. 'It's a trip by ferryboat across the sea to Wyke and then a goodly ride by horse to Melcombe, then a day's ride to yonder town of Dorchester. Even a Portland tern couldn't fly there in an hour!'

Isabel nodded silently as Shamble chuckled and shook his head.

'So where's the King now?' asked Isabel.

'With the Earl of Dorset. This letter ...' Shamble touched the side of his nose, looking secretive, 'concerns the security of the Castle, payments for the gunners, porters and captain there. Deliveries of powder for the muskets. There's cannons and guns there that will keep the Puritans out of Portland. It's an artillery fort, we've got good gunners too. Portland men'll fight till the death for our Castle! And a Groves is never too old to fight neither!' he shouted.

Stella sighed.

Shamble peered at Isabel with his faded blue eyes like the tiny forget-me-knots on the West Cliffs near Isabel's home.

'You after that dog of 'er's, then?'

Isabel shook her head. 'No, I just want to know more about him.'

They all turned to look at Slipknot.

' 'Orrible animal – there's wolf in his blood, I reckon. Folk around Weston and Southwell are saying Stella's tamed the black dog himself!' replied Shamble.

'He's my friend. The Black Dog of Portland is a legend, Slipknot is real,' insisted Stella.

Through the kitchen window Isabel saw the wolves waiting, their yellow eyes fixed on her.

'I have to go,' she said, rising to her feet. Stella nodded.

Shamble poked Stella. 'She's a Maydew girl with them big grey eyes of hers, a local girl, I'd bet my last coin on it!'

'She's from the theatre,' said Stella, daubing Shamble's

arm with her poultice. Shamble and Slipknot watched Isabel as she opened the heavy oak kitchen door.

Isabel left the cosy farmhouse kitchen and walked through the cobbled stables with the wolves running at her heels. The clammy sea mist crept close as the wolves followed her beyond the oak tree at Groves Farm and east along the Giant's Footpath lined with white cowslip. Isabel saw a ring of tall stones ahead of them in the mist, standing in a circle.

'Spooky!' she thought, 'I don't remember seeing them before.' She stopped, reluctant to go closer to the looming stones. The wolf cub scampered to her side and huddled against her, nudging her legs so that his nose stuck between her knees. 'I'm scared too,' said Isabel to him.

The older wolves walked carefully to the edge of the stone circle and sniffed along the ground, waiting for Isabel. She scooped up the small wolf cub and tucked him under her arm. He licked her neck and snuffled her ear. She tip-toed to the wolves, the fog touching her shoulders like the damp hands of old ghosts. Twigs crackled under her feet. 'This is creepy,' she whispered, peering round the dripping wet stones. The mist swallowed up her words.

The large wolf led the way, stepping lightly between the stones into the circle, his yellow eyes wary. The other wolves slipped after him, panting, alert and nervous. Isabel touched a cold stone and stepped into the circle, her ears popping as if she had jumped. Her stomach lurched. The ground felt soft and uneven under her feet. She looked around at the snow-filled circle, small snowflakes drifting down onto her cheeks. They had left the Portland of 1642 far behind. This was the Ice Age, ancient home of the snow wolves. The wolf cub struggled under her arm and Isabel put him down gently on the snow.

In the mists swirling around them, Isabel heard muffled footsteps. A shadow appeared in the fog. Isabel brushed the snowflakes from her eyelashes and looked into the mist. Was it a boy holding a spear? The large wolf tugged Isabel's sleeve, pulling her quickly across the rough snowy ground. She stumbled and fell through the stones on the other side of the circle, leaving the snow, the wolves and the hunter behind her in the distant snowy past.

A football whistled past her ear. Isabel ducked. She was in Grove Park in front of the goal, with snow dripping from her trainers. A group of boys ran past her yelling 'Get out of the goal, Isabel!' She was home again. Isabel sighed with relief.

As she tramped home, Isabel thought about the hunter, a hazy figure in the mist. Her friends the snow wolves had led her there. Isabel wondered why the wolves were showing her this glimpse of the Ice Ages. 'Perhaps it's about the black dog. After all, he's an ancient creature, from the time of the sea dragon and the island giant,' she mused to herself. 'Perhaps he was there in the snow, somewhere.'

The black dog was a mystery and Isabel longed to find out more about him.

CHAPTER TEN

THE MERMAID IS ATTACKED

Miranda crept along the rocks at East Weares near Freshwater Bay, keeping low. The cliffs towered behind her. She had spotted the mermaid and was going to sneak up on her. Piece of luck really. First of all, she had seen the black dog running low to the ground, heading out from Groves Farm. She had followed the animal, but lost it in the mist. Then, for lack of anything else to do, she had followed the surfer Ryder, who seemed to be chasing the dog too. Then the tall, dark-haired boy from Groves Farm had emerged from a clump of trees and joined Ryder heading down to the bay. Finally, she had seen the mermaid out at sea, swimming towards the shore as the sea mist lifted.

Miranda tapped her toe impatiently. She wondered if the black dog had slipped into the sea. He was a strange-looking dog, shadowy and black, not nice and sturdy like Gregor. Perhaps he was not really a dog at all. Perhaps he was an evil shape-shifter and even now was swimming beneath the sea, a giant silver fish. Miranda shuddered. She ducked behind a rock as the mermaid swam in, her dark red hair twirling around her, her long turquoise tail flapping gracefully in the waves. Miranda peered over the top of the rocks, her eyes narrowed. The bright spring sunlight sparkled on the waves. Further south, Ryder was riding a surfboard across the white-topped waves to the rocky shore, skimming lightly over the water. His friend from Groves Farm sat nearby on a rock. Miranda watched the boy curiously.

A glitter of metal caught her eye, just above the sheer rocky cliffs behind the bay.

'What on earth is that?' she yelped, 'Some sort of gun?'

The gun was mounted on a small turret, and a person in a black hat was rotating it slowly. There was a whoosh and a silver arrow cascaded from the cliffs and clanged on the rocks by the mermaid. Miranda heard a distant voice; it was a woman. The mermaid slithered from the rock and vanished beneath the sea, leaving a shimmering circle of water.

'What's that idiot doing?' bellowed Miranda, her hands on her hips. She had missed a fantastic chance to talk to the mermaid thanks to an assassin with a harpoon gun. The figure on the cliffs melted away, taking her weapon with her.

Miranda looked around, her fists clenched, her face scrunched with anger. Still, not everything was ruined. She tottered across the rocks, heading for the dark-haired boy. Miranda flicked her hair happily. She liked being nosy and wanted to find out all about him.

Mrs Groves sat at the kitchen table, her reading glasses sliding down her nose, as she glared at Miranda. 'Can we have more tea, Mrs Groves?'

'That's your third cup,' said Mrs Groves, through gritted teeth.

Her nephew was looking at Miranda as if she were a kind of strange plant, a puzzled frown between his dark eyebrows.

'I'm an expert on the sea. I was watching Ryder surf down at the bay. Of course the Greychurches, my family, are a very old Portland family. So, you're a Groves? It must be great to come and visit.' Gregor lay in his bed by the oven, grumbling gently at Miranda.

'Gregor, hush,' said Mrs Groves, 'I can't think if you growl all the time.' Gregor twitched his eyebrows at her.

'Ha ha, he's a funny dog,' said Miranda, opening the cake tin. Gregor growled even louder. 'There's hardly any cake left,' complained Miranda.

'Shush, Gregor, I don't make cakes for you,' said Mrs Groves.

'I don't really like fruit cake, is this all you've got?' whined Miranda.

Mrs Groves took the tin away from Miranda and put it on the table with a crash. 'I'm sure your mother must be expecting you home by now,' she snapped.

'Oh, I can't go at the moment,' said Miranda, 'I'm desperate to hear all about your nephew.' She leaned her chin on her hand. 'I don't even know your name,' she added, looking dreamily at the boy.

Gregor raised his eyebrows at Mrs Groves as if to say, you're not the only one.

The boy scowled. There were dark rings around his green eyes, Mrs Groves noticed, as if he had not slept for a long time. She wondered why he never talked about his family. She was afraid that the boy had had a difficult life. She and Gregor would have to look after him while he stayed with them.

'Ha ha, names don't matter,' said Miranda, to cover the long silence.

The boy leaped to his feet, knocking the table. Mrs Groves caught her tea cup before it landed in her lap. She sighed, feeling weary. She must go for a walk later in the sunshine when Miranda had gone home. At least Gregor enjoyed his walks nowadays, avoiding bicycles, horses, cars, trees and lamp posts. Also snails. There had been a nasty incident after Gregor ate a snail. He had frothed at the mouth for hours and now had panic attacks if he saw one. Mrs Groves glared at Miranda silently.

'Well, I suppose I must be going,' Miranda said reluctantly.

'You can use the front door, it'll be quicker,' replied Mrs Groves.

Miranda shrugged her shoulders and tried to catch the boy's eye, but he was busy. He had set a pan on the stove and was carefully breaking eggs. She slammed into the dining room, heading for the rarely used front door. It was cold and spooky in the dining room, after the bright sunlit kitchen. Miranda gulped and looked around for the light switch, which seemed to have vanished. There were unlit candles lining the sideboard. She couldn't remember them being there before. The room also seemed darker than she'd remembered. The dark wood panels around the room were creepy. Old portraits of the Groves family looked down at her. Miranda paused in front of Joseph Groves, his portrait dated 1615.

In the far corner, a painting among the Groves women also caught her eye, a small picture of a Stella Groves, dated 1642. It showed a young woman with reddish hair under a white bonnet, who looked uncomfortable in her best pink silks. A large black dog sat in a stately manner by her side, and a sturdy chestnut horse looked over her shoulder. The colours were fresh and bright, as if the picture had just been painted. A vase stood in front of the painting, holding a few small bluebells still sparkling with dew. Miranda squinted at the black dog. She prodded the picture with her finger.

'That's the same black dog!' she exclaimed, 'I must ask Mrs Groves about the painting before I go home.'

Miranda turned to the mirror at the top of the table, pouted and tidied her fair hair in the dusky light. She rubbed her pointed nose, which had gone pink from the sunshine. Miranda froze. In the mirror she saw grey shadows slinking like wolves along the floor.

'Help,' she croaked. She saw glittering yellow eyes reflected in the mirror, drawing closer and closer. Miranda shrieked.

Mrs Groves threw open the door and flicked on the bright chandelier over the dining table. The shadows in the room instantly vanished. Gregor rushed to Miranda, growling and barking. He nipped her leg and shot under the table.

'Ow!' said Miranda, 'He bit me!'

'Nonsense,' said Mrs Groves, 'Gregor never bites.' Mrs Groves looked from Miranda to Gregor, who was sliding towards the kitchen with his belly on the floor. 'Well, he only bites if he's upset,' she said, more truthfully, 'And you did eat the cake.'

CHAPTER ELEVEN

ROBERT GROVES

DEFENDS THE KING

Robert Groves rode Henry, his large chestnut horse, across The Heights heading for the winding track to Underhill, his hat pulled low against the cutting winds that crossed the island from the east. His sword was tucked at his side. Nearing the sycamore trees, he took a sharp left, giving him a distant glimpse of Portland Castle before he rode down to Chiswell, the village near Chesil Beach, where sturdy cottages faced the powerful Chesil waves.

Built during the reign of King Henry VIII, the sturdy fort bristled with cannons to scare off the French and Spanish ships. Shamble viewed the castle with pride. Every now and then he took a swig of brandy to keep the chill out, and he hummed happily to himself an old smugglers' song that his brother Joseph used to sing on a winter's night by the farmhouse fire.

> *We smuggles in lace 'n' brandy 'n' silk,*
> *But women want spices 'n' honey 'n' milk,*
> *Oh it's a terrible life on the sea!*

Far below, the white stones of Portland Castle hove into

view again, the Royal Standard of King Charles billowing in the breeze. Men in gleaming breastplates and helmets raced to the cannons across the curved parapet of the clam-shaped castle. Shamble squinted. His eyesight was not as good as it used to be. He would know many of the local men defending the castle today. Good men. There would be the Combens, the Pearces, the Whites. The old island families stood together. But even from this distance, Shamble could make out smoke and gunshot and boats heading across the harbour from Wyke and Sandsfoot Castle. The forces of Parliament were attacking.

'We'll see about that,' Shamble thought, hauling a matchlock musket with silver fittings from his leather waist belt, 'We'll show them Puritans a thing or two!'

'Mr Groves, wait for me!' Young Richard Lucke rode alongside him and reined in his large black and white horse, his face pale. 'I'm coming with you.'

'What's a young shilly-shally like you doing atop a horse with a bow and arrow? Put those arrows down, you're no bowman,' cackled Shamble.

'I'm coming with you to fight for the King,' insisted Richard.

'Does Stella know about this?'

'She does not,' said Richard.

'Thought not,' chuckled Shamble, 'Very well, follow me.'

He stirred Henry into a canter, riding the long twisting track down to the shore, through the beech trees now springing into leaf and giving them some cover.

'A Groves will never give way to them upstarts in Parliament,' shouted Shamble to Richard, who was struggling to keep up. 'The castle has to stay with the Crown or all is lost! Follow me to Castletown.' The wind whistled through his grey whiskers as he galloped.

They approached the south of the castle. The horses followed the track around the edge of marshland that lay between the pebbles of Chesil ridge and the castle. Shamble pulled up his horse by the moat that protected the fort. Richard rubbed his ears, the cannon shot from the battlements was deafening. Shamble wiped his whiskers thoughtfully. He pulled the letter from his inside pocket.

'Stay out of range of them muskets, lad. I'll distract the varmints at sea while you handle this letter. Hand it to Stephen Hind, the captain, in yonder Armoury. Stay out of trouble, mind, or my daughter will tie me to the oak tree by my boots and hang me upside down for a week.'

Two boats with men armed with flintlocks, shiny tipped pikes and gleaming swords were now a stone's throw from the shore. Shamble and Richard hastily tied the horses and ran through the wooden gatehouse and past the stables. Shielded by the curving wall of the castle, Shamble loaded his musket and fired. A man fell backwards into the sea with a splash. There were shouts and the thunder of cannon fire from the battlements. Musketeers lined the top of the castle and black gunpowder smoke filled the air. Garrison crew ran across the ramparts and the crewmen below loaded the cannons. Avoiding the skirmish, Richard thrust the letter into the hands of a soldier waiting in the Armoury at a narrow cross-looped window.

The man grasped the letter and yelled to him, 'Richard Lucke, thank God! We feared this letter was lost! It has the seal of King Charles himself.'

Shamble ran to Richard's side and grabbed him by the

shoulder. 'Get back to the farm, lad. Your work here is done. My daughter relies on you. Tell her I'm riding out tonight to support the King. I'll find a fisher boat to sail me to Weymouth. The King needs steady men who can show him the lie of the land in Dorset. You've shown proper courage riding here with me today. I'm not against you weddin' Stella, as such. You can ask her, but I reckons she's happy enough as she is.'

Richard nodded, 'I'll ask her then,' he said.

'She knows her own mind, she's the true master of Groves Farm these days,' said Shamble.

There were shots from the battlements and another soldier in the boats fell injured and bleeding into the sea. Musket shot flew past Shamble and Richard as they pressed their backs to the rounded castle walls.

'They'll hold firm here, lad,' said Shamble. 'The Royal Manor of Portland won't bow to the forces of Parliament! Take good care of me daughter. Here, take my sword, these are treacherous times and a man shouldn't be unarmed. That black dog of 'ers isn't all he seems neither, keep an eye on 'im.'

Shamble pulled Henry round and set off at a gallop. Richard watched as he rode towards Chesil Bank, heading for the mainland and the heart of the Civil War. He looked down at the heavy sword and wondered if this time Shamble's luck would hold. Would Stella ever see reckless, brave Robert Groves again?

CHAPTER TWELVE

FIGHT ON THE BEACH

Isabel and Ben sat on the small pebbled Castletown beach in front of the bevelled walls of Portland Castle. Behind them, the tall sycamore trees of the castle gardens rustled in the breeze. Isabel had persuaded Ben to search along the coast of Portland with her and there was still no sign of the mermaid. She suspected that the mermaid was avoiding her. The crescent-shaped castle was overlooked by the blue and white arches of the Sailing Academy. Nearby, tall slender wind turbines twirled in the breeze and the red and white rescue helicopter waited by its hangar on Osprey Quay.

Feeling the eyes of old castle ghosts on the back of her neck, Isabel remembered the battles fought there in Stella's time during the long years of the Civil War. She knew that the castle had been lost and won, that there had been Roundheads in charge, as well as Royalists. The Portlanders themselves had been betrayed by both sides, the castle a valuable prize. Now the low building was like a huge closed clam on the seashore, keeping its secrets to itself.

'I don't believe in mermaids or black dogs,' said Ben sulkily.

'I expect you'll believe in mermaids when you see one,' suggested Isabel.

She gazed across the harbour at the grey battleship *HMS*

Portland, and at the yachts with their fluttering white sails skitting across the harbour. Small waves babbled over the shingle and seaweed near the shore and out at sea the water was dappled blue.

Ben looked at Isabel seriously. 'If you do find your black dog again, what then? He *is* meant to be an omen of death, remember.'

Isabel nodded, 'I know.'

Ben jammed on his MP3 player. 'You should listen to this one, it's *Solar Enemy*.'

His black hair was completely flat where he had taken off his hat, apart from at the front where it stuck up. Isabel nodded, wondering gloomily where to look for the mermaid next.

'That new friend of Ryder's is a bit of a mystery,' added Ben, 'He could be someone famous. Maybe he's hiding out here on the island to escape the pressures of fame, celebrity and *Heat* magazine.'

Isabel nodded, 'Maybe. But I don't think so. My sister Suzie seems to like the pressures of fame.'

'Is he still staying with Mrs Groves?'

Isabel nodded again.

'I might go round later with my guitar. He liked my stuff the other day.'

'Mmm,' said Isabel, tactfully. The dark-haired Groves boy was too quiet. He made her uneasy.

Out on the harbour, she saw a red and purple sail flapping as a windsurfer bounced alone on the harbour waves. He waved to them.

'It's the Surf Dinosaur,' said Ben, and turned up his MP3.

Isabel sighed. She rose to her feet and slithered across the slippery seaweed to the sea, the waves lapping at her trainers. Suddenly the water surged and parted as a cold hand lunged at her ankle.

'Let go!' shrieked Isabel, yanking her leg.

'Useless girl,' hissed the mermaid, emerging from the sea, splashing her long shimmering tail. Isabel struggled, but the mermaid's grip was as tight as steel.

'Why did you try to kill the black dog?' Isabel cried.

The mermaid sneered at her, shaking back her red hair, 'Interfering Maydew! Sstay away from my black dog!'

'He's not yours! He's lived on Portland for hundreds of years!' cried Isabel.

'I've sseen you sspying on me! Beware the black dog, sstupid girl! He'ss a creature of the shadowss, only I can control him!' hissed the mermaid.

Isabel twisted and gripped the striped shell hooked on a thin chain around the mermaid's shoulder.

'Sstop!' screeched the mermaid, releasing Isabel's ankle.

Isabel hung on to the fragile chain. 'You use this shell to call the black dog, don't you, mermaid? Tell me why.'

'Hello, hello!' called a voice from the sea, 'Over here!' Ryder floated in breezily towards them, gliding smoothly across the sea. There was a loud crunch as he hit the pebbles with his board, the sail toppling as he fell forwards on to the beach. He wrestled out from under the sail, draped in seaweed and surveyed them with a delighted smile.

'I expect you were watching my moves out there, Izzie. I won all the local Windsurfing Champs in 1999. Better conditions. Pretty gusty wind out on the harbour today, waves are choppy, could do with a storm at sea. A real stoker!' Ryder looked at the mermaid again. 'Yikes, it's the mer-chick,' he said, backing away and fell with a loud splash into the sea.

A dog walker approached them with a large black and white collie shaped like a fluffy barrel, straining on a leash. 'Slow down, Gregor. Hello Isabel, what a lovely day,' called a familiar voice. 'I see your friend's swimming in the sea, must be chilly. Gregor won't go in the water,' continued Mrs Groves, crunching across the stones towards them.

'Hssss,' said the mermaid, snatching the chain from Isabel's hand.

Mrs Groves stared hard at the mermaid and then blinked rapidly. 'Ah, you're foreign, what a lovely swimming costume,' she said. 'You have trouble with your ess's. I always wanted to go abroad on holiday. We've never been anywhere. Gregor doesn't like travel. Try Speaking Slowly, Dear.'

'Mrs Groves, she's a mermaid,' tried Isabel, edging away from her captor. Gregor had wrapped himself around Mrs Groves' legs and was staring in amazement at the mermaid. His fur stood on end – he looked like a black and white hedgehog.

'Gregor's getting used to the sea,' said Mrs Groves loudly, still blinking at the mermaid. 'He's fine as long as the sea doesn't move. He can't bear things moving around. He's a collie, you know, a very sensitive animal. We're going for a coffee at Osprey Quay.' The mermaid curled her lip, revealing sharp teeth. Gregor tensed.

Ryder crunched up the beach and patted Gregor on the head. Gregor snapped at him but Ryder didn't seem to notice. 'Yeah, I'm great with animals,' he said to Mrs

Groves. 'They love me. I'm in charge of the *Catch the Black Dog* project. Cool.'

'Catch the black dog? That dog could be a wild dog, you shouldn't be trying to catch him, I know a lot about wild animals,' Mrs Groves said angrily.

'The black dog iss mine!' interrupted the mermaid.

'It's all in hand, no worries. I'll catch him for you later, fishy babe,' said Ryder casually.

Gregor growled at Ryder and the mermaid fixed her emerald eyes on Gregor. Gregor snaked between Mrs Groves' legs, his eyes rolling.

'Sstupid dog,' hissed the mermaid.

Gregor pounced on Mrs Groves, who, pulled off balance, crashed into the waves on top of the mermaid, her legs tightly knotted in Gregor's lead. There was a shriek and a volley of furious barking.

'Don't upset him, he's a very nervous dog,' spluttered Mrs Groves, sitting up in the sea.

'Catch you all later,' said Ryder, calmly picking his windsurfing sail out of the sea, shaking off the seaweed and holding up his finger to test wind direction.

Isabel held her hand out to help Mrs Groves out of the sea. Then she froze. Shadows were appearing along the walls of the castle gardens and she felt eyes burning into her. The black dog emerged from the shadows and gazed down at her from the wall, under the dappled green light flickering through the castle trees.

Isabel left Mrs Groves struggling to her feet and ran up the beach to Ben. She tugged his jacket.

'Wha?' he said, taking one speaker out of his ear.

'Let's go! The black dog is over here!' called Isabel,

scrambling up the beach. She clambered over the castle garden wall and stared at the black dog. High above in the sycamores a blackbird sang cheerily and the trees murmured and rustled their flat leaves. A strong scent of lavender wafted around the gardens. Isabel could hear Ben crunching up the beach. The dog gazed back at her, his eyes wary.

'They're all chasing you,' said Isabel, 'Even Ryder! But why does the mermaid want to capture you?' The dog tilted his head at her, as if he understood what she was saying. Isabel crouched down, 'I want to help you,' she said.

'Talking to yourself again?' asked Ben, climbing over the wall. The black dog vanished.

Isabel sighed. 'So you're saying you didn't see him?'

'Nope, didn't see a thing,' said Ben, cramming his hat low over his eyes.

CHAPTER THIRTEEN

CATCHING THE BLACK DOG

Rainbow, the Southwell fairy, was coaching Miranda Greychurch in a quiet glade near Church Ope Cove. Nestled within a cluster of old oaks, the small grove was overlooked only by a sleepy tawny owl. Rainbow sat on a log where toadstools sprouted. She leaned back and toppled into the grass.

'Where are you?' shouted Miranda.

'Here, of course,' said Rainbow huffily, climbing on to the log again. 'Now, take a few steps towards the black dog, then Wallop! Bring the net down. You've got him!'

'Easy,' said Miranda. She was sure she would catch the black dog before Isabel. As soon as she had him, she could make a deal with the mermaid. Then the mermaid would have to toe the line, or tail the line.

'When you've got him, bring him to me. Keep him on the leash. Don't look at him too closely,' added the fairy.

'Isabel won't get a look in,' gloated Miranda, 'I've got it under control. Wallop!'

In fact, thought Miranda, leaning on her net, it was time to wake up the merpeople, drag them into the 21st century. The mermaid was clearly old fashioned. Ocean Park would offer a nice sum of money if Miranda arranged for the mermaid and herself to perform there. Miranda imagined them swimming in circles around the pool with a couple of fish. Not sharks, of course. Perhaps they could catch a nice dolphin or a tuna fish from the sea at the Bill, which they could barbecue after the show and pop into buns. It would be a great success. A sure-fire way to get rich.

'Wall-op,' said Miranda slowly.

All she needed to win over the mermaid was the black dog. Miranda gritted her teeth and pushed her hair back from her pink face. Frankly she could not give two hoots about the dog, but if Isabel wanted him, then she, Miranda, would really enjoy capturing him first. It gave her a warm feeling, a kind of glow. Anyway, it was time she taught Isabel a lesson, the girl got on her nerves. 'Wallop!' she screamed.

Rainbow shrieked and jumped out of the way. She hid behind a toadstool to catch her breath. Still, Miranda was keen and did not ask too many questions. Rainbow sighed. Why did the mermaid want the black dog so desperately? The fairy watched Miranda leap in the air shouting 'Hi-iya!' like a Ninja warrior. Rainbow rested her elbows on the toadstool, while Miranda jumped around, swishing the net. Suddenly it dawned on the fairy. The mermaid was scared, deeply afraid of the black dog. The mermaid had always made threats, deals and promises, but she had never, ever asked for help before now. Not once, in hundreds of years.

Rainbow frowned. It would be best for the fairies if the black dog returned to the mermaid and life continued as before. After all, she and the other Southwell fairies had seen the black dog changing. He was not entirely what he seemed. In fact, they were more afraid of him now than ever before. He was clearly a strange, powerful creature.

Rainbow shuddered. It was going to take more than a Ninja Miranda and a net to trap the Black Dog of Portland.

Mrs Greychurch watched Miranda through her binoculars. Wearing a long black leather coat, she had also pulled on a black woolly hat as a disguise. She rested her arm on the harpoon stand. Her daughter was dancing around with a fishing net. Perhaps it was a new type of folk dancing. Mrs Greychurch scowled. She did not approve of folk dancing. She would have to speak to Miranda about it later. She spun her binoculars over the sea. Was that a tail in the water? She aimed her harpoon carefully.

'Oh yes, my dear, I'll take you out!' There was an explosion and a whoosh as the dart shot out to sea and hit the water. 'Yes!' she shouted. 'Yes, my love, I've got you in one shot! Exit one mermaid!' With trembling hands, she grabbed the binoculars and looked out to sea.

The mermaid dived below the waves, flicking her tail. Mrs Greychurch hissed between her teeth. It was bad enough that the mermaid was out there, circling the island, torturing her. Now she was laughing at her too. Laughing at Veronica Greychurch! She would have to try harder. Perhaps she needed to upgrade the harpoon. Was it sharp enough? If only she had a submarine, she could harpoon the mermaid easily. Even a boat would be useful. Mrs Greychurch narrowed her eyes. She had an idea.

Isabel arrived at Groves Farm stables to ride Isaac. As usual, Isaac was watching for her, stretching his head over the stable door, with a bright eager gleam in his brown eyes. Isabel patted his chestnut nose. Mrs Groves was brushing Gregor in the yard, sending fur flying into the air.

'I'm too busy to ride with you, Isabel. Gregor had his fur trimmed today at the new Dog Grooming salon in Fortuneswell. Will you stand still, Gregor? I can't brush you if you wriggle all the time. Look, here's your new toothbrush.'

Mrs Groves wedged Gregor between her knees and scrubbed his teeth until Gregor frothed at the mouth. 'I'll just fetch the saddle for you, Isabel. Honestly, I never stop.' Mrs Groves tucked the toothbrush in her pocket and bustled away to fetch the saddle, leaving Gregor rolling on his back in a dusty corner of the yard.

Isaac looked down his long nose at Isabel and whinnied, showing large yellow teeth. Isabel patted his neck. She and Isaac often had adventures, with Isaac galloping away with her. Perhaps he would behave himself today.

'Here we are,' said Mrs Groves, 'I'll saddle him up for you, just help me tighten the girth. Gregor! You're filthy! What have you done? Come here!'

Isabel mounted the horse and left Mrs Groves chasing Gregor around the stables with a brush. She rode Isaac across the old cobbles and they set off at a slow pace along footpaths lined with tall poppies and fragrant yellow flowers, heading south towards the windmills. Isaac stepped carefully over the long tendrils of bindweed tangled across the path. Isabel could see for miles in the crystal clear air, the land sloping down towards Portland Bill where the sea currents frothed in the Race. The tip of the red and white lighthouse gleamed against a crisp blue sky. She could hear the rush of the sea against rocks around the coast.

Isabel reined Isaac in to look at the old windmills. 'You've been good today,' said Isabel patting his neck. Isaac snorted at her. From the corner of her eye, Isabel saw a dark shape dart between the windmills. 'The black dog,' she whispered. Lurking behind the nearest windmill was another long dark shadow. Isabel tethered Isaac to a fence post and crept through the clumps of nettles. She pressed her back against the bumpy stone wall of the mill and edged round. Whoomph. A black net descended on her and tangled in her hair. Isabel struggled to free herself, her fingers netted in a tight mesh.

'I'll catch that ridiculous black dog before you!' Through the net, Isabel could make out Miranda's fair hair and angry pink nose.

'Let me go, Miranda!'

Miranda reluctantly lifted the net. 'I nearly had him. One more minute and the black dog would have been mine. You can't bear for me to win, can you Isabel?' Miranda shoved Isabel hard in the shoulder.

'Why are you looking for him?' cried Isabel.

'I was asked, by a Southwell fairy,' sneered Miranda.

'Oh really,' said Isabel, 'So you've been talking to fairies have you, Miranda? I can't wait to tell everyone at school.'

'How dare you speak to me like that!' shrieked Miranda.

She whacked Isabel across the back of her legs with the net.

'Ow, that really hurt! Give that thing to me!' shouted Isabel, grabbing the handle. Miranda wrestled with her. 'He's not a dog, anyway!' yelled Isabel, 'He's a kind of wolf, a rare and very ancient black wolf!'

'He's not a wolf, he's a stupid big dog. And I'm going to catch him.'

A fluffy creature cannoned into them, growling loudly and knocked both of them into the nettles. 'Ow! Gregor!'

'Gracious heavens,' said Mrs Groves from her large black horse, 'Why are you girls fighting? You've upset Gregor. And what's all this nonsense about wolves? We don't have wolves on Portland nowadays. This isn't one of those *Twilight* movies, you know. There aren't werewolves around every corner! Honestly, you young people today live in a fantasy world. When I was young, we were far too busy. We took up knitting or gardening, and read books about otters, owls and lovely lion cubs who were Born Free,' Mrs Groves rambled on.

'I've been stung,' said Miranda, looking at her arms. Gregor licked her face.

'A bit of cream will sort that out,' said Mrs Groves, 'Thank goodness Gregor spotted you. We'll take a slow ride back to the farm, Isabel. Perhaps if you're looking for excitement, we could try a few jumps next time in the field by the farmhouse. Gregor's been practising there. I'm thinking of putting him into the dog agility class at the Cricket Field Fair at the end of the summer, after the police dog event. Several people have said they'd like to see him perform. I always hoped he'd get the Top Class rosette.'

Gregor ignored her, digging a hole near the windmill where he'd spotted a silvery slow worm.

'Stay out of my way, Isabel!' Miranda hissed, stamping off home, clutching her net.

CHAPTER FOURTEEN

MRS GREYCHURCH

HATCHES A PLAN

Mrs Greychurch set up the harpoon in her front room. She felt that the angle of the harpoon was wrong, making her miss the mermaid when she fired. She was also installing the software for her new machine, a small white box that bleeped in the corner of the room. 'Sonar,' she exclaimed with delight. She pressed a button on top of the machine and greenish images came into focus. She sat back on her heels, her eyes gleaming. 'Perfect,' she said.

Neville would be arriving any minute to collect her for a picnic on his boat. How easy it had been to arrange! He had been so happy to hear from her, only saying twice how short of money he was, and three times how he longed for a little holiday paid for by a nice lady like herself.

'I must dispose of that mer-creature. I must focus,' said Mrs Greychurch, as she expertly dismantled the harpoon and popped it into the wicker picnic hamper. She tucked the sonar box beside it. She covered the equipment with a checked picnic blanket, wrapping the edges over two cold bottles of champagne, and stuffed a couple of bananas from the fruit bowl on top. 'There,' she said. She slammed the lid of the hamper and sat on it to close the lid, buckling the straps to hold it tightly shut. She took a small vial of sleeping pills from her handbag and stuffed them in her pocket.

'Dear Neville,' she said, 'He'll sail us to a nice position near Church Ope Cove, then he'll have a lovely sleep. Oh yes, my dear, he will. A Greychurch always works alone.'

She wavered a moment, then remembered the money Neville owed her. A sum she could not afford to lose, £500. Mrs Greychurch hardened her heart. The world of romance was a harsh one and the Greychurches were not forgiving, as Neville was about to find out.

'Are you ready, my dove?' called Neville from the front door.

'Very nearly, my pigeon,' Mrs Greychurch cooed back. 'Come in and help me with the hamper. You have such strong arms.'

Mrs Greychurch pulled green and orange scarves from her sideboard drawer.

'Ah, my angel, you look divine,' said Neville from the doorway. His dyed black hair was swept back from his face and his skin glowed with fake orange tan. He wore a white shirt and spotty pink cravat. Mrs Greychurch sighed as she surveyed him. He was a fine looking man for a 70 year old. Such a shame he was bad with money. Neville checked his watch. 'We must fly, my love. The boat awaits. It's unused to such elegance.'

Neville lifted the hamper, and staggered, his eyes bulging.

'Just a few titbits,' trilled Mrs Greychurch.

'I can't wait,' he gasped. A horn sounded outside. 'Do you have £10 for the taxi? Only I seem to have forgotten my wallet,' he added anxiously.

Mrs Greychurch pursed her lips, 'I'll just write a quick note for Miranda. Hold on to the hamper a moment. Oh dear, where did I put my pen? I'll be with you in a jiffy. Mind you don't drop it. There are fragile things inside.'

Mrs Greychurch dithered and fussed. Finally she propped a note beside the clock on the hall table.

'Oh, I can't wait,' she cried to Neville, as she swept out of the house. She paused briefly in the doorway in her blue stripy shirt and colourful scarves. The taxi beeped impatiently. 'Coming!' she called. Neville staggered behind her.

Ryder was tucking into fish and chips from the chip shop in Weston when the Groves nephew arrived to meet him at Isabel's house. Suzie threw open the door, barging past Isabel as soon as the doorbell rang. She wore a turquoise mermaid costume, with a spiky head dress that stuck out around her head.

'Surprise! I'm a mermaid!' she shouted, 'Oh, it's that strange boy again.' Suzie grabbed him by the hand and pulled him into the kitchen.

'Hello,' said Isabel, as she emptied the dishwasher. She watched him from the corner of her eye. There was something unusual about the boy from Groves Farm. Her mother sat at the kitchen table next to Ryder, singing. She swayed, her eyes closed, as she practised the high, warbling part of the sea shanty, ready for the show at the castle. She had set her hair in big pink rollers and was wearing red lipstick. Ryder had brushed his hair flat, but fluffy bits were already springing out around his head. His salmon-pink t-shirt had been washed so often that the words *Windsurfing Championship UK 1999* had faded.

Still singing, Mrs Maydew plonked a plate of chips in front of the boy. He stared at them, then picked one up and nibbled it. Isabel watched as he picked his way through the chips. She sat down at the table, propped her chin on her hand and studied him. His hair was tousled and his fringe hung over his eyes, like a dark lion's mane. He was rangy, his shoulders broad and strong. He should have been a prince, a warrior prince, thought Isabel. He met Isabel's curious eyes with his own golden-green gaze.

'What's your name?' asked Suzie, poking her head out from under the kitchen table, where she was eating sausage and chips from a tray. The boy opened his mouth and closed it again. Isabel narrowed her eyes, realising that even Mrs Groves never used his name.

'This is Jake, my best friend,' added Suzie. A boy with a heart-shaped face and blonde hair smiled dreamily at them from under the kitchen table. He was also wearing a mermaid dress, with a turquoise skirt that fanned out into a tail, and munching on chips. 'I'm on TV, you know, and Jake is my fan club,' Suzie added, 'I star in the show from Ocean Park about loving little fish. I don't ever eat fish. It's evil and evil people eat them. We never eat them, do we, Jake?' she said, glaring at Ryder.

On the floor beside her was a painted sign, 'No Surffers.'

Suzie thrust it at Jake.

'Hold it up, that's your job,' she yelled, pointing towards Ryder. 'I'm also part of a mermaid rescue thingy,' Suzie added sweetly, 'We're trying to save them from being run down by surfers.'

The Groves boy shrugged, 'I think mermaids can look after themselves.'

His voice was quiet, rather gentle, thought Isabel.

'I've also spoken to the sharks at Ocean Park and they ...' Suzie dropped her tone menacingly, staring at Ryder, '... are watching him.'

'Go back under the table,' said Mrs Maydew firmly. She turned to the boy, 'I hope you're planning to stay at the farm for a bit. Mrs Groves only has Gregor and the horses to boss about and I think she's often lonely.'

The boy looked down at his plate, 'I can't stay at the farm.' He rose to his feet, 'I have to go now,' he mumbled, and rushed for the door.

'Dude,' said Ryder, his mouth full of chips, 'No hassles, I'll finish yours.'

Isabel stood by the kitchen window, pushing back the curtain to watch him walk quickly along the street. From the neighbour's hedges, the snow wolves crept out and followed him. Isabel felt the hairs on the back of her neck prickle. 'Who is he?' she breathed.

CHAPTER FIFTEEN

SLEEPING DOGS

Mrs Greychurch sat at the front of the *Turtle Dove*, Neville's tomato-coloured boat. The wind blew her long scarves behind her as they chugged out of Weymouth marina. The town bridge yawned open, splitting the road into two halves to allow the yachts with their tall slender masts to slide beneath. Mrs Greychurch waved at the people outside the harbour pubs, the first batch of holiday visitors. They motored past The Ship Inn, the fish market and The George on the Melcombe Regis side of Weymouth harbour, finally passing Nothe Fort with its large black guns. Mrs Greychurch surveyed the guns with interest. She wondered if they could be used for her mermaid campaign, and then put it out of her mind. Still, perhaps she could order something a little smaller on eBay to keep at home, just in case.

She gazed up at the *Pelican* tall ship, anchored near the Condor Ferry. She pictured herself sailing away into the night on the *Pelican*, her skirts streaming in the wind. Neville flicked off the engine as they motored into Weymouth Bay and loosed the billowing sails. The *Dove* tilted gently to one side and suddenly all was quiet, just the ripple of wind in the sails. Mrs Greychurch sighed. She could sail forever, it was blissful, relaxing.

'Could you just pull in that rope, my pigeon?' called Neville.

'I don't think so,' she spluttered.

'Of course not, silly of me,' said Neville hastily.

'I should think so too,' said Mrs Greychurch. She tapped the lid of the hamper. 'There may be smoked salmon in here,' she trilled. Only there wasn't. Just a harpoon and sonar. And a couple of bananas. 'I've a surprise for you,' called Mrs Greychurch. She produced her other secret weapon from the hamper, two bottles of champagne.

'My favourite,' cried Neville, delighted.

'I know,' said Mrs Greychurch grimly, 'They cost a fortune. Now open this bottle would you, there's a dear.'

'If you could just take the tiller?' ventured Neville. Mrs Greychurch glared at him. Neville wedged the tiller against his knee, sending the boat in a large loop while he wrestled with the bottle. It opened with a loud pop.

'Bottoms up!' shouted Mrs Greychurch, catching the champagne in a fluted glass into which she had already crumbled a sleeping pill.

They sailed past the Portland Breakwater, the *Dove* skipping over the waves. As they rounded Portland, heading for the eastern side of the island, Neville sipped his champagne.

'Very fizzy, isn't it,' he hiccupped.

'None for me,' insisted Mrs Greychurch, 'I've another bottle to open later, to celebrate.'

They cut close to the Isle as the small boat sailed past The Grove, with its low sandy cliffs and lines of trees.

Neville smiled at her. 'Fuzzy fizzy,' he said.

'Have another little sip,' cooed Mrs Greychurch. The

Cove was not far away now. She needed to get rid of him.

'Think I'll harve a little naarp,' slurred Neville, his head already lolling to one side, his eyes closing.

'Good idea!' said Mrs Greychurch. As Neville rolled forward, she kicked him firmly into the cabin and locked the hatch. 'Done and dusted,' she said smiling, rubbing her hands. She steered them towards the bay at Church Ope, took down the sail and tossed the anchor into the sea. This was the ideal spot. She had a clear view of the Cove, with its grey rocky beach. Small waves lapped around the boat, rocking it gently. Mrs Greychurch was sure the mermaid was nearby. In fact, she faintly heard a thin voice singing not too far away.

'La li la,' trilled Mrs Greychurch, 'Now for my lovely harpoon.' She whipped the harpoon out of the hamper and put it on the deck, fitting the pieces together expertly. She connected up the wires that ran the sonar and dropped the transmitter into the sea, watching the luminous green screen. A shoal of fishes passed below the yacht, clearly visible on her screen. 'Perfect,' she said and sat back to wait for her victim, the mermaid, one hand resting on the harpoon, ready to fire.

Mrs Groves relaxed in the lounge. She put her glasses on her nose and opened the *Dorset Echo*. Gregor roamed the room, unsettled. There were shadows in the corners with yellow eyes, like wolves waiting at the edge of a camp. He was uneasy and it made him hungry. He tugged a cushion from the sofa and rolled on the rug chewing it. Mrs Groves snatched the cushion and replaced it on the sofa.

'Sit down, Gregor, for goodness sake, just let me relax for 5 minutes. I've been on the go all morning, you've had two walks,' she grumbled. Gregor looked at her blankly and scratched the door. 'You naughty dog, you went out 10 minutes ago. Why won't you sit down and be quiet? Where's your squeaky bone? Why don't you chew that?'

The squeaky bone was under the sofa, ripped to shreds, the squeak eaten. Every now and then it made a funny noise in his tummy. Gregor sniffed the base of the door, making loud snuffly noises and whined. 'Go out then.' She let him out and waited in the kitchen. A few seconds later, there was a gentle scratch at the door.

'Come in,' called Mrs Groves, opening the door. The black dog padded into the kitchen. 'Oh my giddy seashells, it's you!' she gasped. His fur was gleaming and he looked strong and well fed. 'Someone's been looking after you.' The dog gazed back at her with wistful eyes. 'What a magnificent animal! What shall I feed you?'

She opened a cupboard and fished out a bag of dog biscuits which she poured into a bowl. The black dog ate a few, watching Mrs Groves out of the corner of his eye as she pottered around, making tea. Then he curled up in the corner of the kitchen on the warm tiles by the stove and fell into a deep sleep. There was another scratch at the door. 'Oh no. Gregor,' said Mrs Groves. She looked nervously at the sleeping dog, his breathing deep and peaceful. Gregor would go berserk.

Mrs Groves tiptoed to the back door and opened it very slowly. Gregor's nose shot through the gap and he glared at her. She grasped his collar and edged him through the kitchen door. He looked around wildly, sniffing, as he sensed an intruder. Gregor bayed like a pack of hounds and threw himself across the kitchen at the black dog, with Mrs Groves hanging on to his collar. They grappled with three kitchen chairs, which crashed to the floor. Two plates from the drainer by the sink collided with Gregor's tail and smashed against the wall. The cup from the kitchen table shattered, splattering the walls with tea. Finally, Mrs Groves and Gregor wrestled on the floor enwrapped in the checked table cloth. 'Naughty boy, will you be quiet,' she hissed, sitting on him.

Gregor, surprised, stuck his head out from under the table cloth. He had lost his sense of direction. Mrs Groves shoved him into the lounge with his tail between his legs. She leaned against the door, panting.

Amazingly the black dog was still asleep. After watching him for a few moments, Mrs Groves followed Gregor into the lounge where she found him curled up, sulking in the middle of the rug, his eyes staring accusingly at her. They glared at one another until she picked up the *Echo* crossword.

'Hmm, *Dark God*,' she read the clue aloud, 'Two words, Gregor, five letters and three letters. I don't know that one. *Polite Fight in 1642*, two words, five and three letters again. Heavens, they make these questions hard.' She put her feet up on the foot rest and closed her eyes. Her nephew came in quietly from the kitchen and sat opposite her in the armchair. Gregor snored loudly. The nephew picked up the paper and filled in the letters carefully.

Mrs Groves opened one eye. 'I didn't hear the outside door open, it normally creaks,' she said.

The boy shrugged, 'Not always.'

'Hmmm,' said Mrs Groves, drumming her fingers on the arm of her chair. She tottered to her feet and peered in the kitchen. As she suspected, the wild black dog had gone and the door was closed. She looked at the boy again. Perhaps he had let the dog out. 'Will you give me a hand with the mucking out tomorrow? I want to chat to you about staying on at the farm. Gregor and I could feed you up a bit. You could go to college in Weymouth. It would do you good to settle down. We can write to your parents tomorrow. D'you have an address for them?'

The boy shook his head.

'Don't worry,' said Mrs Groves. 'I expect they'll get in touch at some point. My parents were like that too. I was sent away to school. I'm afraid a lot of the Groves are hopeless with children.' Gregor woke up suddenly and jumped to his feet, barking. 'I could use some help with Gregor and running the farm. Will you stop licking my toes, Gregor! He can help with your training.'

'Hrrumph!' said Gregor.

'I have to go,' said the boy, rising to his feet and heading for the door.

'Gregor will enjoy a walk with you later,' called Mrs Groves after him. 'That boy's a fidget, never sits still,' she added to Gregor, 'I think he has things on his mind.'

'Hrrumph,' said Gregor again, settling for another nap.

CHAPTER SIXTEEN

WIND IN THE SAILS

As the evening drew in, the *Turtle Dove* was still anchored in Church Ope Cove, the sea swell rolling the boat peacefully from side to side. The small bay swept in a curve of grey pebbles, surrounded by oak and chestnut trees that hid the ruins of St Andrew's Church. Rufus Castle perched over the cove to the north. It was a fairy-tale bay, sheltered from the winds that cut across the sea from the Atlantic west. Mrs Greychurch shook her head foggily. She sipped her drink again.

'I need to pull myself together,' she thought, woozily. 'I must have drunk too much champagne.'

She glimpsed the turquoise sheen of the mermaid's tail out at sea. She narrowed her eyes and swivelled the harpoon on its pivot, staggering slightly.

'Bleep, blip-bleep,' went the sonar.

'Die mermaid, die,' she said between gritted teeth. Mrs Greychurch held her breath and fired into the gloom.

'Missed!' she exclaimed in disgust. She sipped her drink again and popped it on the hatch. Or was it her drink? Mrs Greychurch looked at the glass with a sinking feeling in her stomach. Both glasses, hers and Neville's, were now rimmed with lipstick. 'Oh dear,' she said as she nodded off, sliding on to the deck.

'Hello, hello!' called Ryder, windsurfing towards the boat across the cove. 'Anyone on board?' He peered down at the usually immaculate Mrs Greychurch, snoring like a stranded walrus on the boat deck.

'Hi, Ryder,' called the boy from Groves Farm. He was sitting on a large grey rock nearby, his hand trailing in the sea. 'Good breeze this evening. A south-westerly, d'you reckon?' he asked.

Ryder surfed over to the rock. He frowned, thinking about the wind, an obsessive glint in his eye. 'Or is it more of a westerly?' he debated, 'Could be south-south-westerly, with a touch of westerly. Or is it southerly, veering westerly? I need to catch the black dog, gotta get my best surfboard back, dude.'

Mrs Greychurch hiccupped peacefully on the boat. Below the hatch, a thin voice called across the waves, 'Hello?'

Ryder looked around wildly. 'Funny, thought I heard a voice.' He pointed up at the mast of his windsurfing board. 'I used to know a bloke who had a weathercock on his mast for wind direction. Not much use. No, this is more of a westerly, I think, turning north-westerly later. Not so great for wave riding tomorrow.' Ryder's shoulders sagged under this crushing thought. 'I'm glad you asked about the wind, though,' he added, leaning against the mast with his arms folded, as if it were a lamp-post. 'Wind causes waves. Now, local winds create messy waves, close together, no good for windsurfing. What you need is a big storm over the Atlantic to give a good strong swell. Then you need the wind to blow *faster* to make big waves. If it blows *longer*, you get even bigger swells. Perfect for windsurfing.'

The boy smiled. 'The islanders used to stand on Pulpit

Rock and raise the waves by singing to the spirits of the sea, the mer-people. The storms would bring the best fish close to the land and people would dive into the sea and spear the fish,' he said.

Ryder raised his bushy fair eyebrows. 'Never tried that myself,' he mused.

'It was a while ago, there aren't many mer-people left,' added the boy. 'Will you teach me to windsurf?'

'I'm a great teacher, dude, the best, you can count on me to show you some cool moves. I'll lend you a board and take you through some forward loops.'

'Is that what beginners do?' asked the boy.

'They do with me,' insisted Ryder.

They both looked at the bobbing red boat, anchored in the bay close by. 'I'll swim out and help her,' said the Groves boy, 'She's asleep, I think.'

The boy dived into the sea and swam to the boat. Ryder raised his eyebrows again. The boy swam like a merman, flexing his legs as if they were a powerful tail.

Once on board, the boy hauled up the anchor and switched on the engine. 'I'll motor the boat round to the harbour,' he called, as the boat chugged. He waved to Ryder who was still testing wind direction, his hand waving in the air.

Ryder toppled backwards into the sea. 'Definitely more south than south-westerly,' he spluttered, bobbing in the frothing waves left by the small boat.

Isabel gazed up at the first stars of the April night as she walked along the dusty track near Groves Farm. Above her, the towering constellation of Orion the Hunter was trailed by the Hunting Dog. He reminded her of the tall, mysterious Groves boy with the snow wolves at his heels. Mrs Groves roared past her along the track in the muddy Land Rover with Gregor panting out the window, his ears blown back by the wind. She stopped with a screech of brakes.

'We're late for the knitting club, Isabel. I'm afraid my nephew's out if you're calling on him. Must go!'

Isabel waved as Mrs Groves drove off, the wheels spinning on the dusty track. At the top of the hill, the stout outlines of the ruined windmills loomed ahead. Two white horses startled her, galloping across the fields in the twilight like silver unicorns. As Isabel followed the Giant's Footpath across the heart of the island, the small towers seemed to sneak closer to her. Isabel looked at the ivy-clad circular buildings. Mrs Groves called one of them the Angel Windmill, although she'd never explained why. In the distance, she heard a wolf howl. It was getting late. She dug out her mobile and called home.

'WHAT?' bellowed Suzie down the phone.

Isabel held the mobile away from her ear. 'It's me,' she said, 'Tell mum I'll be home soon.'

'OK,' shouted Suzie, slamming down the phone.

Isabel walked around the windmills, avoiding the prickly thistles and clumps of stinging nettles that thrived in the windswept fields. Another wolf howled, closer this time. The sky was shifting colour from dark blue to indigo, and the planet Venus glittered in the south, as bright and cold as a diamond. She felt knots of excitement in her stomach as the wolf howled again nearby. The snow wolves were coming for her again. Isabel stood very still, hardly breathing.

From the star-lit south, the pack of wolves bounded across the fields, leaping the bramble bushes. The large grey and white wolf reached her first, his tail bristling. He crept forward, tugged her sleeve and pulled her along with the pack. Isabel looked for the wolf cub, who bounced to her side, his nose caked with mud. Together, they ran across the field as the first flakes of snow puffed into Isabel's face. They splashed through pools of melting ice, the wolf cub bounding along on his sturdy paws, into the snowy wilderness of the Ice Age Isle. Isabel slipped in a huge puddle, landing hard on her bottom. Soaked, she scrambled to her feet and looked around, the wind moaning in her ears. She was alone. The wolves had gone and there was a giant dark figure looming over her.

With huge spokes like wings reaching high into the heavens, the windmill stood over the Portland meadows like a guardian angel. 'The Angel Windmill!' gasped Isabel, 'Where am I now? The ice and snow have gone too!' Isabel looked around, searching for the familiar lights of Groves Farm to the north. She heard the heavy tramp of boots and ducked behind the windmill as a troop of soldiers marched towards her.

CHAPTER SEVENTEEN

SOLDIERS AT GROVES FARM

Stella was woken suddenly in the dead of night by Slipknot tugging at her bed covers. 'What is it, boy?' she asked, sitting up. The dog darted from the room and ran down the creaky wooden staircase and through the long hall to the kitchen door. Stella followed him on tiptoe and opened the door. 'Isabel!' she exclaimed, 'What are you doing here in the middle of the night?'

Isabel, soaked and out of breath, pushed at the door. 'Quick, you have to bolt the door, there are soldiers,' she cried.

Stella pulled her inside and slammed the kitchen door.

'This won't hold them,' she said, her voice shaking.

Isabel glanced through the window. The group of soldiers trudged across the yard near the barn and outhouses. Above them, clouds fluttered like huge feathers through the night sky, and pale moonlight glinted on a metal breastplate, helmets and a pike, glittering evilly.

'Up here! We can hide in the attic,' called Stella from the top of the stairs.

She led Isabel to the attic stairs that wound up into the farmhouse roof. They crouched in the shadows. 'Slipknot, come with us!' Stella whispered loudly. The dog bounded up the narrow stairs and Stella rested her hand on him.

They listened and waited.

Heavy leather boots clattered across the cobbled yard.

'They're soldiers, but not the King's Cavaliers. I reckon they're seeking out my father,' Stella whispered. She stood on tiptoe to peep from the tiny attic window. There were just seven men with dark sashes across leather tunics, carrying swords as well as flaming torches. 'They're as young as me, staggering with them great swords! Dorset lads, I'd say, called to fight for Parliament but scared out of their wits.' The tallest man with a plumed hat banged his fist on the heavy kitchen door.

'Open up!' he barked. When no-one answered, he shouted menacingly, 'You'll pay for your treachery against Parliament!' and they heard thumps against the oak door. Slipknot crouched low between Stella and Isabel. The door burst open with a crash and soldiers paced through the farmhouse. Stella and Isabel heard the swish of a sword as curtains were ripped.

Isabel felt Slipknot's dark eyes on her. 'No, stay with us,' insisted Isabel, resting her hand on his head, 'There's nothing you can do.' The black dog gazed at her.

'Slipknot trusts you, Isabel,' whispered Stella. Isabel nodded.

'I'm not afeared of a bunch of boys!' Stella slipped into the darkness of the attic and rummaged under the eaves. 'Look, my Uncle Joseph's sword!' Stella pulled the heavy sword a little way from its tarnished sheath and looked at it nervously. It was clammy to touch. Her uncle would have made short work of scared young soldiers with it.

Suddenly the darkness in the attic seemed to draw closer and Stella dropped the sword with a clatter. The golden eyes of a pack of wolves blinked at Isabel and Stella. 'Waah!' shrieked Stella, scooping up the sword and waving it wildly.

'Don't be afraid,' whispered Isabel, 'The wolves want to help us.'

'Where did they come from?' wailed Stella, backing against the sloping walls of the attic, 'Are you a witch? Did you conjure them with an evil spell?'

'No!' cried Isabel, 'Stop shouting, Stella!'

'I'll shout if I want to!' she yelled. 'There's lads ruining my curtains downstairs and a pack of wolves up here! Who are you, Isabel? Are you a Maydew witch?' Stella swiped the sword at her, hitting the eaves with a loud clang.

Isabel ducked and shoved Stella sideways, knocking the sword from her hand. 'Stop waving that sword around!' she shouted.

Stella grabbed Isabel by the hair and yanked her to the dusty floor, slapping her across the ears. 'You're a witch!'

'Ow!' cried Isabel.

'Why are you fighting?' asked a low voice. A tall figure stood over them. Stella opened her mouth to scream and Isabel stuffed her hand across Stella's face

'Shhh! Don't be afraid,' the boy said quickly.

Stella pushed Isabel's hand away from her. 'We're not afraid! Where in heavens did *you* come from? I've never known such a strange night.'

Downstairs, soldiers pushed over furniture as they searched the rooms. Isabel stared at the strange boy in the thin trickle of moonlight from the attic window. His tousled dark hair fell to his shoulders and he wore a simple robe of animal skins. He shivered.

'For goodness sake,' said Stella. She crawled to the corner of the attic, pushing past wolves, and rifled through a heap of garments in the corner. 'Put this cloak on, stranger. At least you can be dressed when you invade my home,' she said, draping the large wool cloak around the boy. She looked nervously at the wolf next to her, 'I reckon the soldiers may do us harm. They seek my father, Robert Groves. He carried a message to the men at old King Henry's Castle. Now he's gone to fight for the King.'

The boy picked up her uncle's sword. He admired the sharpness of the sword edge.

Stella put her hands on her hips, 'Who are you?' she demanded, 'Are these your wolves?'

The boy held up his hand. 'Listen,' he hissed.

'Nothing down here,' a young soldier declared at the foot of the attic stairs.

'They were forewarned. The farm is empty. Burn it down. Those drapes will fire easy,' an older voice commanded. Stella and Isabel held their breath.

'Wait,' another voice said, wavering a little, 'I heard something.'

A burning torch lit the foot of the attic steps. 'Oh no,' thought Isabel.

The boy left their side and stepped into the light, holding the sword ahead of him. He kicked the torch from the soldier's hand, sending it spinning and plunging them all into darkness. The wolves poured from the attic, with the men fleeing ahead of them, confused and shouting. Stella gripped Isabel's arm as they ran down the attic steps, almost tripping over her when Isabel stooped to pick up a pike dropped on the floor. Isabel bounced the pike in her hands. It was heavier than it looked, strong wood tipped with iron.

Stella snatched the long pike from her, 'I'll take that!' she said, ''Tis my farm after all.'

Stella rushed past the boy, who was wielding the heavy sword with surprising grace. The soldiers were crammed into the main staircase, their faces pale with fear, surrounded by snarling wolves. At the foot of the stairs below them stood Richard Lucke, gripping his own gleaming sword.

'What's going on?' he yelled. He reached out and gripped one of the soldiers by the collar, 'Where's Stella Groves?'

'I'm here,' called Stella from above.

'Are you harmed? I heard a commotion from over yonder. And who's this?' Richard pointed at the tall boy.

Stella looked the boy up and down quickly, 'A friend, come to help us.'

'And wolves?'

'Yes,' said Stella in a squeaky voice, 'It's been a strange night here, Richard.'

A soldier tugged Isabel's arm. 'What is this place? This Isle is full of dark magic and terrors! We heard tell of it over in Portesham where we live. They say Portland's protected by ghosts, witches and men who sling stones that take your head off!' shuddered the soldier. 'We said we weren't fightin' no Portlanders, but we were ordered here tonight.'

'Portland'll always hold for the King,' said Richard. 'You boys should leave now before the wolves do you harm!'

The soldiers clattered down the stairs and ran from the farmhouse through the broken kitchen door. The man in the plumed hat stopped and sneered at Richard.

'Your tricks don't scare me,' he said, 'Whatever magic and

witchery brought these wolves here to aid you tonight, it will not keep Portland from the rightful hand of government. The island will yield to law and reason in the end. The old days of kingly rule are over – now the people will rule for themselves.'

Stella ran down the stairs, waving the pike. She jabbed the man in the plumed hat with the iron tip. 'Don't threaten us. Portland will not stand for an invasion! Chase him far from here, into the sea,' she said to a wolf.

The soldier fled into the night with a snow wolf in pursuit.

With a last glance at Stella, the tall boy left and the rest of the wolves followed him. Richard walked into the shadowy stable yard and watched them disappear into the darkness under the Groves oak tree. A very strange night, he thought. Surely wolves had not lived on Portland for hundreds of years, not since the days of the Norman kings, William and Rufus. He wondered if it was true, that Portland had no chance of holding on for the King if the rest of England fell. Richard sighed, there were dark times ahead.

Stella picked up her uncle's old sword, left propped against the kitchen wall. The boy had gone, with his magical wolves. A mysterious boy. Stella shook her head, a little disappointed. She would have liked a better look at the wolves, with their golden eyes and silvery fur. Stella marched to Richard in the yard, where the horses shifted restlessly in their stables, and stood with the sword at her side.

'The Groves always fight back,' she announced proudly.

'They do,' said Richard, smiling at her.

Stella looked around the deserted yard. Even Isabel had

vanished. The farm felt strangely empty.

'Oh no, Slipknot's gone!' she cried, 'He's never left my side before!'

'Perhaps he runs with the wolves now,' suggested Richard.

'Yes, perhaps,' said Stella wistfully, 'I think something was calling him. He was like a restless ghost at night. Many times I've heard an eerie cry at dawn that made my blood run cold. I've a feeling he'll search for Isabel. He trusts her. My father was right, she's no theatre girl. Magic happens around her. I hope she'll look after Slipknot.'

CHAPTER EIGHTEEN

STAR GAZING

Isabel ran after the boy from the attic. 'Wait for me!' she called, 'I know who you are. You're Mrs Groves' nephew!' panted Isabel.'

The boy disappeared beyond Groves oak tree, the snow wolves trotting at his heels. Isabel lost him completely in the deep forbidding darkness of the 17th century Isle. She stopped and looked around, deciding to head east where the sky was lit by dazzling stars. She cut along a track, the ground deeply rutted from carts laden with Portland stone, leaving dust strewn across the deep grooves. Her shoes became snowy white with soft chalky dust. She turned onto an overgrown footpath by small dark cottages with tiny windows and low thatched roofs. A large imposing building loomed ahead, with tall glittering windows like a cathedral. Listening for the sea, Isabel turned and zigzagged down steep, narrow pathways towards the water. In the gloom, she saw the outline of Rufus Castle, the sturdy Keep overlooking meadows that sloped down to the east coast. Isabel heard the sea lapping at the shore, the waves lit by sparkling pinpricks of starlight.

Isabel looked out across the sea. She felt the large snow wolf brush across the back of her legs as he joined her. Isabel crouched down with him, glad to have found a friend, her hands in his thick fur. 'Have you come to take me home?' she asked.

Light flakes of snow began to tumble from the sky, making her shiver. Isabel looked over her shoulder. Along the coast, huge cliffs of ice rose up and gleamed with an eerie blueish glow. She stared at the sheer precipice. High above her, the ice jutted out like a forehead. Two closed eyes overlooked a noble ice nose and a wide mouth, like the frozen face of a slumbering giant. Small streams of melting ice water gushed over the cliff, streaming down his frozen features. Isabel put her hand to her mouth, mesmerised by the sleeping giant. Gentle snowflakes covered her head and shoulders. But then, like a sudden blast of icy wind, Isabel felt time shift around her. The ground fell away under her feet, a block of ice crumbling into the sea. She felt herself falling backwards, spinning over and over, the snowy blizzard stinging her eyes. She threw out her arms, expecting any second to plunge into the icy sea.

Isabel landed lightly, rolling on her back, as if she had been caught by a giant hand. She opened her eyes. The wolf stood by her side, shaking the snow out of his fur. She could hear a familiar sound, a whirring noise. The lights of the Portland rescue helicopter blinked overhead, flying over the island on a rescue mission. Isabel breathed out, glad to be back in her own time. She stretched out her arms and legs and looked around. The Groves nephew sat on the uneven sandy ground with the pack of snow wolves, looking at her curiously.

'Did it hurt when you fell from the sky?' he asked. Isabel shook her head. The boy frowned. 'You appeared from nowhere,' he said.

Isabel knelt by him and the wolf cub rested his head on her knee, looking up at her and snuffling her hand with his wet nose. His bristling white whiskers tickled. She stroked his head, ruffling the soft fluffy fur between his ears and he wagged his bushy tail. The other wolves sat by the boy, looking up intently at the stars, their tongues lolling from their mouths. Over the boy's shoulder, Rufus Castle loomed, its walls crumbling into a sheer drop.

'Did you travel across time too?' asked Isabel.

The boy shook his head, 'No, I was here.'

'But you saved Stella and the farm in 1642! You were there, I saw you! You fought the soldiers with the old sword from the attic,' Isabel cried.

The boy nodded, 'I do remember, but that was a long time ago,' he said. The boy held his hands out in front of him and flexed his strong fingers. Above them, stars glittered like tiny diamonds. The constellation of the powerful Star Dog bounded across the sky.

The boy looked up at the stars. 'D'you know the constellations? The Celts used to say that the island giant put the stars in the sky to map out our fate.' He pointed, 'That's the Hunting Dog constellation. The star nearby is called *Sirius*, the brightest star of all, the Dog Star.'

Isabel gazed up, 'I can see a galaxy up there in the Hunting Dog, like a yellow flower, a sunflower.' Isabel pointed to a small spiral of golden stars. Her voice rang as clear as a church bell across the sea, where the mermaid listened, her eyes as cold as the distant stars.

The boy nodded, 'That star in the Hunting Dog is called *Cor Caroli*, after King Charles I. He was executed by his people and Oliver Cromwell ran the country as the

Lord Protector. The islanders fought for the King, but the Roundheads took Portland Castle, and many folk have walked the castle walls since then.'

The boy turned to Isabel, his eyes glittering, 'It's strange you're not afraid of me. But I suppose you don't know who I am. You set the sea dragon free and you weren't scared of him either. Now you travel across time with my friends the wolves, seeking out the past, asking questions about the Black Dog of Portland. What did you see when you travelled into the past?'

'I met Stella Groves at the start of the Civil War in 1642,' said Isabel, eyeing him nervously. She was not frightened, but there *was* something strange and otherworldly about him. And what did he mean, she didn't know who he was? Was he a secret time traveller? A friend of the black dog? 'I also saw the Isle of Portland covered in ice,' she continued, 'Where the snow wolves used to roam, thousands of years ago. I'm not sure why the wolves take me there. There are giant cliffs of ice and snow blizzards.'

The boy clenched his hands into fists and looked away from Isabel. 'I know why. The wolves want you to know how it began, the story of the black dog. Perhaps they think you can help him, but he's not like you or Mrs Groves, he's a wolf, the black dog.'

He jumped to his feet, his shoulders tense with anger and fear. Below them in the bay, with a tiny splash, the mermaid disappeared into the sea. Isabel stood up and looked at the rings spiralling outwards on the still water. She wondered about the mermaid and her hand in the black dog's fate. She turned to the boy, 'I'm not sure who you are, but you're a friend of the snow wolves. We have to do everything we can to help the black dog.'

Isabel's mobile rang, the sudden noise shrill in the silence around Church Ope, making her jump.

'HURRY UP! YOU'RE IN TROUBLE!' shouted Suzie, 'DINNER'S READY!'

Isabel hurried to the steps leading from the Cove. She paused and looked over her shoulder. 'By the way, what's your name? Everyone calls you the Groves nephew, but you must have a name.'

The boy held her gaze with his dark green eyes. 'Wolven,' he said at last.

Isabel's mouth fell open. She froze. Images flashed in front of her. She saw the black dog with vivid green eyes on West Cliff, the tall boy in the attic, and Stella's friend Slipknot. She stayed very still.

'Now I really *do* know who you are,' Isabel said quietly, 'And the mermaid knows too. You're the black dog.'

CHAPTER NINETEEN

WOLVEN REMEMBERS

The following day, as dawn lit up the island, Wolven walked up the narrow path through the Weares, cutting past beach huts nestling in the steep hill above the Cove House Inn. He looked down at the cottages of Chiswell and the long golden stretch of Chesil Beach. Sea thrift grew among the rocks at his feet. As the wind tousled his hair, he breathed deeply and closed his eyes, letting the air run through him. He heard the faint echo of the firelit drums of the past, driving out the ice gods with old magic and bringing in the new era. He longed to be free of the past, skimming across the sea like the windsurfers on Portland Harbour. Free as the kestrel hawks that hovered over Hamm beach along the shores of the Harbour.

He looked down at the powerful waves sweeping across Chesil Bank. The shores of the Isle were battered year after year by powerful waves, storms following calm, sweeping the past away. He watched the undertow sucking the pebbles into the sea. In the distance, he heard the mermaid blow into her conch shell, calling him. He stooped and curled his fingers around the tiny yellow orchids, rooted into the ground. He wanted to stay at Groves Farm and help Mrs Groves. He felt like he belonged there. He did not want to be the black dog any longer.

Feeling the dew on his fingers, he remembered the thaw that came at the end of the Ice Ages, leaving grassy hills and bubbling streams. He remembered moonlit nights, when the early settlers followed the tracks to the south of the Isle, holding fiery torches. He ran alongside them, a lone black dog, and the stars sparkled over them.

Later he saw the tall gracious Romans, the fair-haired Saxons and the Viking invaders, who tumbled ashore from huge longboats at Church Ope Cove. He saw the Giant's Castle fall into ruins, and Rufus Castle built in its place. He admired the temple to Venus under the stars in the east, with spirals carved into the white stone pillars. The same ancient stars still twinkled down on him at night, the Hunting Dog stretching across the heavens behind Orion the Warrior. The black dog often gazed at this constellation, wondering if his fate had been written up there in the skies.

Would Mrs Groves think he was a monster if she knew his secret? After all, Isabel was not afraid of him. The boy wiped his eyes on the back of his hand. Perhaps he should tell Mrs Groves the truth.

It was early in the morning, barely 6 o'clock, and lines of orange and lemon sunlight stretched low across the eastern sky, as the sun rose behind strands of wispy cloud. A distant aeroplane drew a frothy line across the deepening blue of daybreak. Mrs Groves stood at the kitchen door, her arms folded, watching the plane vanish as the sun rose. She had travelled very little. The farm had always kept her busy. She looked proudly at the stables and the meadows where the older horses grazed peacefully. She worked hard to keep the farm up to scratch and she was proud of her work, but she had always hoped, one day, to see a bit more of the world.

Gregor was curled in his bed, fluffed out and irritated. His paws were chilly with Mrs Groves lingering by the door, creating a nasty draft. He was not an early riser and disliked the dawn, especially the silly tweeting birds and soggy grass under his paws. Much better to go out later when it was dry, for a long walk on the beach at Portland Castle where lady ghosts smiled at him from the battlements and exciting things happened.

Gregor yawned and slunk out of his bed, gulping Mrs Groves' toast with barely a crunch. He peered around her legs at the yard, sniffing the morning air. He cast a resentful glance at Mrs Groves and scuffled outside to sniff around the corners of the yard. Finding a gap under the shed, he dug around in the dirt with his paws. He was sure a nice fat mouse lived under there. It would be good to chase it. Mrs Groves sank into the kitchen chair by the door, lost in thought.

'I think we need to get out more, Gregor,' she called. 'Don't dig over there! Your paws will be filthy! It's time we spread our wings a little. If my nephew's staying with us, we can travel to Holland on the ferry. We can eat exotic cheese. We can buy clogs and look at tulips and canals.'

Gregor ignored her. He shook out his damp fur and sniffed around a bit more for the mouse, keeping a wary eye out for early morning snails. Mrs Groves leaned her chair back against the door frame, her thoughts hundreds of miles away. Gregor gave up on the mouse and snails, and slipped by her into the kitchen, leaving a line of muddy paw prints across the kitchen floor. He shook again, sending damp splatters of mud around the room. Bored, he chewed the edges of the doormat. After spitting a few soggy pieces on the floor, he turned his attention to the tea towel. He tugged it down from the stove and spent an enjoyable 5 minutes ripping it to shreds. By the time Mrs Groves returned from her daydream, he was making serious work of the table leg, grinding his teeth into it, his eyes closed blissfully.

'Bad dog!' shrieked Mrs Groves. She snatched an old towel and chased him around the kitchen. 'Let me wipe your paws! What's wrong with your chewy bone?' she cried. 'That's it! We're going on holiday!'

At that moment her nephew arrived home, wandering into the kitchen and tripping over Gregor as the dog hurtled for the dining room. Mrs Groves noticed that he had dark rings around his eyes. She touched his shoulder lightly, surprised at how cold he felt, as if he had slept in a cave.

'I'm going to vacuum and tidy up a bit. Gregor's been misbehaving. I'll have to brush him, then I'm going to nip out,' said Mrs Groves. She must speak to Mrs Greychurch about a holiday. There was a lot to do.

The boy nodded. 'I'll see to the horses for you,' he said.

Mrs Groves tugged the vacuum cleaner from the cupboard under the stairs, a large metal beast from 1977 when Mrs Groves had bought it brand sparkling new.

After several repairs over the years, it now made a noise like a fighter jet taking off. Mrs Groves stamped on the start button and the machine vroomed into life. Gregor shot on to the sofa and hid under a cushion as Mrs Groves trundled around the room, dust spraying sideways from the machine.

The vacuuming done, she grabbed Gregor's fluffy brush and comb from the windowsill. Gregor tried to squeeze behind a chair. 'Got you!' she bellowed. She caught him by the collar and hauled him outside, fur flying.

Wolven returned from the stables to an angry but smooth-looking Gregor, curled in his bed. He eyed the boy and harrumphed. The boy found Mrs Groves in the dining room, dusting around the paintings. 'That's Joseph Groves over there,' she pointed out. 'You look a little like him, you have the Groves nose. Of course, your name is ... ahmm ...'

'Wolven,' said the boy.

'Wolven, of course,' said Mrs Groves, nodding her head. Wolven pointed to a smaller portrait of a red-haired girl.

'She was a fine woman,' said Mrs Groves. 'My great, great ... I lose count ... grandmother, Stella Groves. She ran the farm for many happy years with her husband Richard Lucke.'

Wolven smiled.

'Yes, she was a remarkable Portland woman,' continued Mrs Groves, noting that her nephew rarely smiled. 'Her grand-daughter wrote a diary. She tells the story of a black dog that Stella kept before she married. My other favourite tale is how she frightened a troop of soldiers at the start of the Civil War and saved the farm. She was completely fearless. You must read it. She's always been a family heroine.' Mrs Groves hesitated. 'So, will you stay? Have you made up your mind?' she asked nervously.

Wolven looked into Mrs Groves' anxious eyes. His mouth was dry. 'The black dog that was here ...,' he began, his voice shaking.

'Yes, I think he's a wild dog. If you find him, bring him back. I'd like to offer him a home at the farm. The poor animal wanders the fields of Portland alone and needs proper food and shelter. Animals need to be cared for, no matter what they are,' said Mrs Groves matter of factly.

Wolven made up his mind. He nodded, 'Yes, I'll stay at the farm.'

Pleased, Mrs Groves returned to her dusting.

Wolven looked at his hands and frowned. Stars flashed in front of his eyes. He flexed his fingers. Something was different. Like a sea mist on an April morning, the enchantment lifted. He saw puzzling memories, from a time before he was the black dog. He remembered running across a cold island through melting ice, a spear in his hand. Wolven put his hand to his forehead, trying to stop the memories that rushed at him like a giant wave. He had been the chief's son, a tribal prince; crouching by a fire, listening to stories, hunting wild hare, fishing in the rock pools. Wolven clenched his fists. As he left the farmhouse, he kicked the statue of the mermaid and the dog, smashing it into tiny pieces.

Beneath the ground, within layers of limestone, the island giant stirred in his sleep. He turned to face the sky, the ground rumbling and shaking, cracks running across the grass as if a small earthquake was shaking the island. He opened his eyes, tumbling two beach huts against one another. Above him, beyond the pale blue sky, he saw the stars spin like patterns in a kaleidoscope. He frowned, tracing their paths, seeing all the things that had happened since he last awoke, hundreds of years before. He stretched his arms within the land, feeling underwater springs rush through his veins. He uncurled his fingers and the ground rose with his deep breath.

The island giant lifted his fingers from the land and wove time around them in a spiral. The stars twisted into a new pattern as he bent time and space like the gentle curves of a snail shell. He saw the boy, a tribal prince, by the rocks and the mermaid waiting there. He saw the shadow of the lone black dog running across the fields, night after night. He tapped the Hunting Dog constellation lightly with one finger. The tiny stars rearranged into the figure of a young man holding a billowing sail. Slowly, the giant fell back to sleep, with the ancient island of Portland in his arms.

CHAPTER TWENTY

NO MORE MERMAIDS

Miranda Greychurch cycled through the sunlit village of Southwell, where clusters of primroses bloomed by the roads, looking for the mermaid. She was fed up. She had wasted days searching for the black dog. She had nipped on to the computer and done some research. Black dogs were scary, dangerous, evil demons with glowing eyes. Miranda swerved her bicycle at the roundabout, narrowly missing Mrs Groves and Gregor in the Land Rover, and took the winding road that led south to the tip of the island where she would start her search for the mermaid. The wind howled in her ears as she rode past the Culverwell fields where Stone Age people once lived, heading for the red and white lighthouse.

A Southwell fairy, of course, would make a good exhibit at Ocean Park. Miranda gritted her teeth and crouched low on the bicycle, furious that she had not grabbed the fairy. She cannoned past the Old Lower Lighthouse. She hated the Maydews. She should be on TV in the *Sea Life Special* as a local mermaid, instead of that awful Suzie Maydew who hogged the limelight at 6 o'clock on the show every week. She rode hard, pedalling faster and faster. She whizzed past the car park, the cafe and lighthouse, turning a sharp right, and headed for Pulpit Rock. She took the sandy track that led along the ancient rocky beaches of the Bill. At the last moment, Miranda screeched her brakes. Nothing happened. 'Yeeeow!' she yelled. She hurtled down the rocks into the sea, head over heels, and splashed into churning sea water. As she struggled to right herself, she felt the current pulling her out.

'Sstupid girl,' hissed the mermaid, appearing in the sea. 'I've enough problemss. Now I'm sstuck with you again!'

'My brakes didn't work!' yelled Miranda, clutching a rock where the sea broke in stinging foamy waves up her nose.

The mermaid swam beside Miranda. 'You have to let go of that rock and sswim to the sshore.'

'I can't,' gasped Miranda.

'Don't be ssilly,' said the mermaid. She sighed. It was time. 'Ssister, take my hand, thiss iss your last chance. I'll show you shipwrecks filled with treasure chessts, the cave where the ssleeping ssea dragon lies, wonderful fish ...'

'Ugh, get lost, I think I've a phobia of fish. Oh no, something just touched my leg! Was it a fish? I think I'm going to scream! Aaagh!'

The mermaid splashed sea water into her face. 'Sstop it!'

'The sea's ruining my hair,' wailed Miranda. 'There's seaweed touching me now! I feel faint! I need something to eat.'

'We're natural creaturess,' hissed the mermaid. 'We eat fissh.'

'There's no way I'm eating fish out of the sea. You'll have to send my mother to the fish and chip shop.' Miranda let go of the slippery rock and clutched the cold mermaid, gasping in her ear, 'Get me out of the sea. I don't want to go anywhere with you anymore.'

'Promisse you'll never bother me again,' hissed the mermaid.

'Yes, I promise! Not this week anyway!' shrieked Miranda.

The mermaid hauled her towards the shore, swimming hard against the strong current and flexing her tail, tugging a heavy Miranda. She dumped her by the rocky beach and swam north around Pulpit Rock and along the shore. At the picnic tables, a newly arrived coach party watched as she swam past.

'Did you see that, Terry?'

'Must be a new thing, some sort of show.'

The coach party wandered into the restaurant for a cup of tea. Meanwhile, Miranda clambered out of the sea, flicking seawater angrily. She plodded towards the cafe, where Mrs Groves and Gregor had pulled up at the mini-roundabout.

'Are you all right, Miranda, d'you need a lift? We're on our way to the Co-op,' called Mrs Groves. Miranda got into the car and slammed the door with a loud bang.

When Isabel arrived at the Groves' farmhouse later that morning, she found Mrs Groves in the kitchen unpacking her weekly shop from the Co-op while Gregor snaffled in the green recycled bags, sniffing loudly.

'Get out of there, you naughty dog! That's not for you!'

Gregor sank his teeth deeply into a red apple, which looked like a ball. His teeth got stuck and juice dribbled down his furry chin. He whined and shook his head.

'Take it off him, Isabel,' sighed Mrs Groves, stuffing boxes of dog biscuits into the cupboards. Isabel tugged at the apple and wriggled it from side to side until Gregor's teeth pinged free. Gregor shook himself and glared at Isabel.

'You can take Isabel outside to throw your ball for you,' said Mrs Groves, 'I can't play with you all the time. I've been on the go all morning. I had to drop Miranda off. She's had an accident on her bike. I never get time to sit down.' Gregor barked and bounced towards the door.

'I'm looking for your nephew, Mrs Groves,' said Isabel quickly.

'Wolven went out earlier. He has a windsurfing lesson with Ryder,' snapped Mrs Groves. 'Gregor can help you look for him. Here's his lead. Off you go. I'll collect Gregor from you this afternoon at your mother's concert.' Mrs Groves hustled them both to the door and shut it firmly behind them.

CHAPTER TWENTY ONE

MERMAID ENCHANTMENT

Isabel waited uneasily at Church Ope Cove on the mermaid's favourite rock, her feet dangling in the cold green sea, her socks stuffed into shoes next to her. She was afraid the mermaid would try to sneak up on her, may even attack her, but it was a risk she had to take. Isabel splashed her toes in the sea and shivered, keeping a careful eye on the waves that rolled towards the Cove. A sea mist drifted across the water like smoke and in the distance she heard singing, a thin horrible sound. Gregor snuffled around the stones on the beach. He found a piece of old cuttlefish and settled down to chew it, glancing at Isabel's shoes. He planned to chew one of those in a minute. Isabel looked out to sea, determined to wait for the mermaid and try to discover what she knew about Wolven, the black dog.

There was a splash behind her. Isabel jumped and looked over her shoulder. A shoal of silver fish swam by. Isabel felt fingers drumming slowly on the rock, icy mermaid fingers. She turned to find the mermaid staring up at her, the glossy tendrils of her tail fanning out in the water. Her glassy eyes were narrowed and she hissed. Isabel quickly curled her bare feet out of the sea and tucked them under her on the rock.

'You know about Wolven. You have to talk to me,

mermaid!' exclaimed Isabel. 'I saw you last night. You were watching Wolven.'

The mermaid plunged beneath the waves and, with a powerful flick of her tail, flipped on to the rock beside Isabel, sea water pouring from her glowing white skin. 'Thiss rock was once a sstone in the wall of a ssea fortress, from the time of the island giant.' The mermaid stroked her fingers across the silvery-grey rock, 'Carried from Atlantiss.'

Isabel leaned forward and looked the mermaid in the eyes. 'Tell me about Wolven,' she insisted. 'Someone needs to know his story, before it's too late to help him.'

The mermaid smirked. 'He belongs to me, I found him a long time ago. The glaciers were melting into the ssea. The mammoths and reindeer went north into the ssnow. I wass left behind, alone.' The mermaid flicked the edge of her tail, splashing salty water into Isabel's eyes.

'Ow!' cried Isabel, rubbing her eyes on her sleeve.

The mermaid caught Isabel's wrist in a steely grip. She smiled a slow menacing smile, her face close to Isabel's, her sharp teeth gleaming. 'Bring me Wolven, and I'll tell you everything you wissh to know,' she hissed. 'I'll sshow you the secretss of time travel. And you may go where you wish, ssee whatever you choose. I'm your friend, Issabel.'

Isabel pulled away from the mermaid, looking at the blue imprint of fingers on her arm.

'What was he when you found him, a black dog or a boy?' she asked.

The mermaid smiled and ran one cold finger down Isabel's cheek, gazing into Isabel's light grey eyes. Isabel shuddered.

'Why doess that matter? He'ss a werewolf, a vicious

creature. Bring him to me and all will be well, Issabel. You can trusst me. He'ss dangerous, wandering losst around the Isle, he may harm ssomeone. He belongss to me. He'ss the Black Dog of Portland.'

Isabel sat in silence for a minute. She thought about Stella Groves and the Angel Windmill with its sails stretching to the skies. To explore the island of the past was her dream. She could trek through the end of the Ice Ages with the snow wolves, meet the Romans and Vikings. But then she looked into the mermaid's cunning green eyes. 'No,' she said, 'I don't believe you. Wolven wants to be free of you, mermaid.'

Isabel scrambled over the rocks, leaving the mermaid hissing angrily behind her. She scooped up her shoes, one of them chewed and wet. 'Gregor, come on!' Gregor scampered to her side and jumped up at her, his paws soaked from paddling in the sea.

CHAPTER TWENTY TWO

THE CONCERT

Mrs Maydew tapped the microphone with her finger. There was a shrill whistling noise that echoed through the thick stone walls of Portland Castle, through the Great Hall and Courtyard, waking the ghosts from their slumbers. Gusts of wind blew across the harbour into the circular castle garden and tugged at her gold earrings. The show was due to start at 6 o'clock but they were already running late. She was dressed as a pirate, with a striped scarf over her hair and a gold waistcoat. She hummed into the microphone and sang a few bars of a song. Isabel put her mother's bottle of water next to the stool.

'I hope that's a bottle of rum,' sniggered her mother. Isabel rolled her eyes. Gregor jumped up at Mrs Maydew and licked her face.

'Get down, Gregor,' said Isabel wearily, tugging at his lead. It had been a long afternoon. After they had left the beach at Church Ope, Gregor had eaten a worm, been sick, fallen in the garden pond and broken a vase of daffodils. He had also eaten two packets of Rich Tea biscuits, including the wrappers.

Ben was setting up the sound system and microphones, trailing leads backwards and forwards across the grass from the amplifiers to the speakers. Behind the pine trees, fairy lights around the walls of the castle garden were flickering on and off, cutting out the stage lights.

Suzie, with the camera crew for the *Sea Life Special*, was dressed as a spotted conger eel with a long trailing tail. She posed on the steel and wood bridge that led to the garden, surrounded by bluebells. One of the crew held a silver disk to bounce light into her face. She perched on the rail, doing a piece to camera.

'Many fish come out when it's dark. You aren't going to be eaten if a sharkie can't see you. That's a fish fact.' She gazed at the camera. The director noted 'Fish Facts' on her clipboard.

The lights suddenly flashed off again. Gregor dragged Isabel across the bridge towards the castle, bumping past the camera crew, chasing a pretty fluttering creature.

'Isabel! Get him off!' gasped Rainbow, crash landing among the bluebells. Gregor sniffed at her suspiciously. 'Your dog smells funny,' she added.

'He fell in the pond,' explained Isabel. Gregor looked from Isabel to Rainbow and back to Isabel again. He was having an interesting day, with lots of walks and plenty of new people to meet and greet. He snuffled the fairy again and decided not to eat her. His stomach ached.

Rainbow sighed, 'Isabel, the black dog's a werewolf.'

'Why d'you think that?' asked Isabel.

'Well, he's part human and part wolf, so he must be a werewolf!'

Isabel shook her head, 'I don't think so. He's just a person most of the time.'

Gregor gave the fairy a gentle wet lick.

'Ugh!' complained Rainbow. She flipped backwards over

the wall and vanished.

Isabel looked over the garden wall towards the sea. She saw Ryder on the shingled beach in front of the castle, next to the line of colourful boats. He was taking off his harness and balancing the boom of his windsurfing board on the stones, the blue and red sail flapping in the breeze. 'Be right with you, just getting my guitar,' he called up to Isabel. He unstrapped the guitar case from the front of his board and galloped up the beach to the stage in the garden to join the sound check, dripping sea water over the speakers.

Ben grabbed Isabel's arm as he rushed past. 'Were you talking to a moth?'

Isabel sighed, 'It was a fairy.'

'No way!' said Ben, 'It was a Silver Studded Blue, you can only see them on Portland, they're very rare.'

'Ben, have you seen Wolven from the farm today? I've searched everywhere for him.'

'Wolven? Is that his name? He'll show up later, I invited him. Gotta dash,' said Ben, adding, 'Where's SD? Surfing Dinosaur, I mean. I could do with a hand. The electrics are on the blink. Oh, there he is.'

Isabel patted Gregor. He panted at her happily. She climbed on to the garden wall and trailed her eyes across the harbour. Mrs Greychurch clunked past her with a large holdall, which she put down near the castle with an ominous thud, and there was a familiar thin wail from the sea, the haunting seashell call. Isabel saw the sparkle of a turquoise tail some way out. She jumped down from the wall.

'That was the cry of a lonely mermaid, a very rare sea mammal found here in the harbour,' called Suzie. 'Someone better go and give 'er a hug. Where's Isabel? Come here, Izzie. By the way, that's another Fish Fact, so write it down,' she said to the director with the clipboard. Suzie grabbed Isabel's shoulders. 'Lift me down from the bridge, Izzie, we can go to the beach and show the camera crew a real live sea mermaid.'

'Not now, Suzie,' cried Isabel. Over Suzie's shoulder, she saw a boy running along the shore. 'Wolven!' she exclaimed

Ryder looked up from his guitar, 'Hey, is that the black wolf? Someone's keen to get her fins on him. And I need my board back from the fishy babe, urgently!' He propped his guitar by the speaker.

'Here, Suzie, look after Gregor!' said Isabel, hurriedly thrusting Gregor's lead at Suzie. She left them looking at one another and ran through the castle gates, jumped the stone wall on to the beach and landed with a crunch. Ryder followed her.

In the sea, near the breaking waves, the mermaid was waiting, the conch shell in her hand, her glowing skin silhouetted against the dark blue sea. She pointed at Wolven. 'If you want your board, capture him for me!' she called. Ryder hurtled past Isabel and made a flying tackle at Wolven, missing him completely and skidding on his stomach into the sea like a penguin. He landed with his nose close to the mermaid's tail.

'Listen, fishy dude, I can't find that wild black dog, he's too slippery. And I can't hang about chasing Wolven either. Got a show to do. Can I have my board back now? It's an original *Catch the Surf* board.' The mermaid hissed.

Twinkling lights flickered on and off in the garden,

reflected in the mermaid's glittering green eyes. Strange screeches echoed across the harbour as Ben adjusted the sound system. In the aura of shimmering lights and sounds, Wolven and the mermaid faced one another. Wolven held a long spear whittled from a holly branch, with a sharp flinty point. To Isabel's surprise the mermaid recoiled, curling her long fingers over a mark on her arm. Wolven tested the spear in his hand. 'I should have killed you all those years ago, weird creature, neither human nor fish,' he snarled.

Ryder looked from the mermaid to Wolven, then from the mermaid to the spear. He backed out of the sea. 'Wow, this is a bit hectic, Izzie. I'll just grab some chips from the burger van in the car park over there near the castle and be back in a minute. Let me know what happens.' He ran up the beach, his shorts flapping around his knees.

'I remember everything!' Wolven spat at the mermaid, 'You turned me into the black dog. It was you! An evil enchantment!' The point of the spear glinted as Wolven drew back his arm.

'No, wait!' cried Isabel, 'Mermaid, it's time to explain what happened to Wolven. And tell the truth this time!'

'Never!' cried the mermaid. She lunged at the boy and dragged him into the water. Isabel dived after them, trying to pull Wolven free of the mermaid's ice cold grip.

'He attacked *me*!' snarled the mermaid, holding the boy's throat. She plunged his head under the water. 'Sstabbed me through the arm with his sspear. It wass an easy enchantment. The dog wass in hiss heart, after all. It wass his destiny, written in the stars by the island giant!'

The boy struggled free, raised his spear from the sea and held it over the mermaid.

'Wait!' cried Isabel, 'Why did he attack you?'

The mermaid slid away from Wolven into the waves. 'He wass the son of a chieftain. I saw him by the rock pool with his friendss, the wolves.' The mermaid flexed her long white fingers. 'He wass clever at catching fish. I had pearlss for him, from the oysterss in the sea. But he attacked *me*! A mermaid, a rare precious creature! So I made him hiss true sself, the Black Dog of Portland.'

'I'd never seen a mer-creature! How was I supposed to know she was evil, scheming and cruel?' glowered Wolven.

Isabel looked from the mermaid to the boy. 'Wolven, the mermaid's afraid of you,' she said, 'You attacked *her*, remember?'

'She enchanted me!' Wolven shook the sea water from the spear and the mermaid flinched. 'But now I've changed,' he said, 'The enchantment is over. I pity you, mermaid, *you* can never change.'

The mermaid shivered and splashed her long tail in the water. 'Maybe not. My life iss hard,' she admitted, 'I have no power. People on the island no longer respect and fear me, not like in the old dayss when I dragged them sscreaming into the ssea. Thosse were happier times.'

Ryder ambled back down the beach towards them, stuffing chips in his mouth. 'What happened?' he interrupted eagerly. 'Did she say where my board is? Did anyone get killed?'

'I should drag you into the depthss of the sea, usseless human being,' hissed the mermaid, lunging at him.

'Woww, that's a bit sudden, let me finish these chips first,' said Ryder.

The mermaid backed away in disgust. 'Don't come near me. Your board liess behind a rock at the Red Pool, near the lighthouse,' she hissed. She twisted in the sea and flipped her tail, her eyes on the horizon, where the sea melted into the sky. She cast a final glance towards the boy, as if for a moment she was unsure of herself. Wolven glared back at her angrily, his knuckles clenched white around the spear. Isabel sighed. She had hoped the truth would free Wolven from the past, but now that seemed impossible.

CHAPTER TWENTY THREE

THE FINAL ATTACK

Isabel watched as the mermaid began to swim out towards the harbour. The lights around the castle had failed and on the beach they were plunged into a cool indigo darkness. At Isabel's side, Wolven and Ryder also stood silently watching the mermaid swim away. Isabel glanced at Wolven. He caught her eye and shrugged, his face cold and angry.

There was a clattering sound from the castle behind them. Suddenly a harpoon zinged overhead attached to a long silver wire. Horrified, Isabel gasped as the glistening arrow arced over them towards the sea.

'Mermaid! Look out!' she cried. The mermaid turned to glance over her shoulder at Isabel as the arrow plummeted towards her. She stared up at it and raised her arm. She shrieked. Like a shooting star, the arrow fell from the sky.

'The arrow's hit her!' yelled Isabel. The mermaid tugged at the harpoon, sinking helplessly below the dark water.

On the castle ramparts, above the black cannons that jutted from the walls, Mrs Greychurch rotated the harpoon and took aim again. Wolven stared at the injured mermaid. Barely hesitating, he plunged into the sea and swam after her. As she slid deeper beneath the waves, he lifted her above the sea and, in one swift movement, pulled the arrow free. Isabel and Ryder flattened themselves on the beach as another dart flew overhead. At the last moment, Wolven turned. The arrow struck his shoulder. He floundered in the sea, gripped the spiked arrowhead and yanked it free.

'I'll stop her! She's reloading!' cried Isabel.

'Too late!' gasped Wolven, 'You won't get to the castle in time. I'll take the mermaid out to sea, where she'll be safe.'

He looked down at the mermaid, who floated with her eyes closed on the breaking waves, her face sickly pale, clutching her arm. 'Strange, for so many centuries I longed to be free of her. But people have never understood mermaids. She has no power over me. I can't leave her.'

'Hurry up!' shouted Isabel. 'She's going to fire again! I'll run up to the castle. She's on the upper gun platform!'

Wolven was by the mermaid's side, lifting her head above the water, where she gasped and shivered. 'Are you badly hurt?' he mumbled.

'It'ss not the first time I've been attacked,' the mermaid snapped, struggling. 'Let go, sstupid wolf.'

'I'm trying to help you,' snarled Wolven.

'I don't need your help,' argued the mermaid, 'I need to sswim out to sea, where it'ss peaceful.'

'Fine, I'll swim out with you,' growled the boy.

'Hey, take the fishy babe out on this,' called Ryder, clambering to his feet on the beach, with chips in his hair, 'I left my windsurfing board here on the beach earlier, I ran a bit late. It's a perfect evening for a bit of wave sailing. You did ok this morning, Wolfie, with your windsurfing lesson.'

'My name's Wolven, and I nearly died,' said Wolven, wading back towards the shore with the mermaid, 'Beginners don't start with backward loops.'

'Yeah, they do when I teach them,' said Ryder. 'You were great, Wolfie. A possible for the Olympic windsurfing team, I'd say. It may surprise you but I'm a bit too old to try out for the team myself. But I could train *you*. I'd say you have *star* potential.'

'All right,' said Wolven warily, 'Later.'

Ryder looked at Wolven's shoulder. 'It's fine, a flesh wound. I've windsurfed with all kinds of injuries. It was 1998, I was down at Kimmeridge Bay ...'

'Get on it with it,' snapped the mermaid. Ryder and Wolven draped the mermaid over the front of the board and Wolven stood unsteadily on the slippery white surface, trying to find his balance as he tugged at the sail.

'Yeah, you've got it,' called Ryder. 'Turn the sail this way. Now check out wind direction. You might need to gybe a bit.'

'What?' called Wolven, over his shoulder.

'Yeah, use a carve gybe in a downwind turn, scissor the board a bit. Gotta go, Wolfie, they're waiting for me to play the guitar.'

Wolven leaned back and tugged the boom, angling the board to catch gusts of wind in the sail. 'I think we're all right, with a southerly wind I can sail out of the harbour and around to the east of the island.'

'Take me to the cove at Church Ope,' ordered the mermaid, draped uncomfortably across the board. She placed a piece of seaweed on the wound.

'Does it hurt?'

'Of course it hurtss!' The mermaid glanced up at Wolven. 'There are few of us old creatures left,' she said sadly.

Wolven tugged at the sail, feeling the flow of the wind. 'I

shouldn't have harmed you, mermaid,' he admitted, 'Now my life is starting once more. The dragon sleeps, the ice has melted and finally I'm free. I'll always have the black dog in my heart but I'm Wolven Groves now.' The mermaid hissed and stared at the southern horizon, remembering the old days.

They surfed steadily across the harbour, bobbing over the waves, and cut through the Portland Breakwater, heading for the east of the Isle. Reaching the castle gate, Isabel saw them sail away. She shuddered, hoping that Wolven would keep a close eye on the treacherous mermaid. As dusk fell, Isabel looked for the stars. She could usually pick out Venus, a slender crescent of a star. Mars often appeared at dusk too, a tiny pinkish globe. Isabel ran towards the castle under the first stars of the evening.

Mrs Greychurch leaned on the thick castle wall next to the harpoon, squinting at the sea. Darkness was creeping in rapidly and she could no longer see the mermaid in the water. The sea was an inky blue. She should have brought her glasses. Still, she was sure she had hit the mermaid with the first shot. She was satisfied with her work. She dusted off her hands and laughed wildly.

'You sound happy, Veronica,' said Mrs Maydew climbing the stone spiral staircase. 'Have you seen Isabel? Or Ryder? The audience is getting restless and we need to start the show.' Isabel ran up the steps behind her. Mrs Greychurch stared coldly at her.

Mrs Maydew took Isabel's arm, her bangles jangling. 'Now that you're here, Izzie, you can organise Suzie. She's finished filming for the *Sea Life Show* and I think she's been drinking Coca-Cola.' Over in the gardens, Suzie was spinning on a stool, whizzing around in circles, her conger eel tail swirling after her. Her friend Jake was pushing her faster and faster. Gregor was fast asleep next to her, partly dressed in a mermaid costume, a blue tiara on his head.

Isabel tugged at the harpoon. 'This thing is dangerous!' she said to Mrs Greychurch, 'I'm taking it apart.'

'You young people don't know anything about weaponry. Leave it to me,' said Mrs Greychurch, shoving Isabel out of the way. 'Now, this bit unscrews here.' Mrs Greychurch took apart the harpoon pivot and folded it on top of her bag as Ryder played the intro to the first song.

'That's me! I have to go!' Mrs Maydew rushed down the steps from the battlements, across the bridge and into the gardens, where she joined in with a ballad called *Tale of the Olde Sea Dog*, smashing a tambourine against her leg to mark time.

Miranda Greychurch arrived at the castle and bounded up the castle steps to them, elbowing past Isabel. 'What's that?' she asked, staring at the harpoon.

Mrs Greychurch smiled at her daughter and puffed out proudly. 'You will be thrilled to hear, Miranda, that the Greychurches have once again saved the Isle of Portland!' She patted the harpoon, resting in several pieces on her holdall. 'I, alone and unaided, have harpooned a mermaid.'

'Mother!' shrieked Miranda.

'Yes,' said Mrs Greychurch, 'I can see you're impressed. We Greychurches can't stand mermaids, and you'll be very pleased to hear we're no longer infested with them here on the island.'

Isabel glared at her. 'Infested?' she exclaimed.

'Well, I suppose it's for the best,' said Miranda, a little pale. 'But what am I going to do now? I'd made plans for the mermaid. I'll have to do GCSEs. What a pain. I've hardly started the folklore project for History, and it's due in after Easter.'

'Folklore, load of rubbish,' snorted Mrs Greychurch, 'All that nonsense about black dogs with glowing eyes and silly Southwell fairies!' Mrs Greychurch smoothed her hair. 'Help me pack up the harpoon,' she added. 'Oh, and I've some more good news for you, Miranda. We're going on holiday with Mrs Groves, to Holland, with Gregor! Isn't that fantastic?'

Isabel giggled at the horrified look on Miranda's face.

'Oh no, not Gregor!' cried Miranda.

'What an interesting song,' called Mrs Groves, appearing with Gregor at her side, his paws slithering on the smooth parapet. 'Gregor loves it. He had a fantastic time with Suzie. I had to take off his mermaid outfit as his paws got tangled and he kept tripping over. Is this a *Motorhead* song? I've never heard this version of *The Ace of Spades* before. Every day there's something new.' She beamed at Miranda and Isabel.

Gregor sniffed happily at Miranda and licked her hand. 'Yuck,' said Miranda. 'My day really can't get any worse.'

'Neville's paid me back some money,' said Mrs

Greychurch. 'He said he was afraid I would kidnap him again! The silly-billy! Now you can buy some clothes for the trip, Miranda.' Miranda cheered up.

'Well, I guess chasing the mermaid was getting a bit boring,' she said to Gregor, ruffling his fur. Miranda pictured herself in clogs, walking by the canals, in a big checked dress ... with Gregor.

'We can take the ferry from Harwich to the Hook of Holland on Stena Line. Pets travel free!' said Mrs Groves. 'Gregor will love the ferry. He may get a little sea sick ...' Gregor whined and shook out his black and white fur. 'My nephew'll take charge of the farm while we're gone. I know I can count on him. Gregor and I have become very fond of him. He's part of the family now. We remember his name, Wolven of course, a very old Groves name.' Gregor whined again. A ghost lady in a pale bonnet and a faded lavender dress kept trying to stroke his ears. It made him nervous.

Isabel smiled to herself as she left them and ran down the winding castle steps, across echoing rooms that had seen nearly five centuries of Portland life; Cavaliers and Roundheads, the storms of war and calmer years of peace. She ran through the whispering sycamore trees to watch the show.

CHAPTER TWENTY FOUR

SHAMBLE RETURNS

It was close to midnight when Robert Shamble Groves walked up the path to Groves Farm. He paused every now and then to look over his shoulder. From time to time, he thought he saw a pack of grey and white wolves flitting through the trees to the south.

'Blasted wolves, 'orrible things,' he said, his hand resting on his sword as he looked around.

He remembered an old song his mother used to sing to him when he was young. About a lonely mermaid, who enchanted a boy and turned him into a black dog. He gazed up at the stars, humming to himself. With a stubby finger, he traced their familiar shapes.

'Sirius, the Dog Star,' he said, 'Now, where's the Hunting Dog? It's vanished. I don't recognise that constellation, a hunter, I'd say, like Orion.' He had sailed many oceans and knew the stars very well. But this evening he was puzzled. 'Some sorcery afoot, I fear,' he muttered to himself.

Shamble shook his head. As he strolled by the sprawling oak tree, he noted that the farm looked different tonight, brightly lit with yellow lamps in the parlour. No flicker from candles. He frowned, pausing at the kitchen door, which stood ajar. It was built from some new light-coloured wood with a small diamond-shaped window. He tiptoed into the kitchen. One eye peered around the dining room door, followed by a fluffy ear, as Gregor stared at him.

'Hello, who are you then, you big rascal?' cried Shamble. He ruffled Gregor's fur and threw open a kitchen cupboard. 'Stella's moved the brandy again! What's this stuff?' He took a swig of sherry. 'Bit sweet,' he said, wiping his mouth on his sleeve. He put the bottle into the deep pocket of his long dark coat, pulling out the bluebells he had picked on his way through the woods. He plopped them in a jam jar and left them in the middle of the table. Gregor whined. He had hoped for a biscuit.

Shamble leaned over and held Gregor by the ears. 'Now then, young fellow, you look after the farm for me. I'm off to France on a smuggler's ship. She waits for me down at Church Ope, ready to sail at dawn. I'll have some tales to tell when I get back!'

'Hello,' called Mrs Groves. 'Who's there?' She pottered into the kitchen in her dressing gown, her glasses sliding down her nose. Gregor looked up at her, twitching his eyebrows. 'What's up with you, silly dog? It's your bedtime.' There was a cold draft from the back door, as if a ghost had just left. Mrs Groves shivered and closed the door. On the table in the empty kitchen was a small bundle of bluebells in a jar.

'Oh!' said Mrs Groves, 'Gregor, where did these come from? Have we had a visitor?' She took them carefully from the jam jar and carried them to the dining room. She put them in an antique vase on the sideboard, in front of one of her favourite paintings, of her ancestor Stella Groves.

Isabel carried Suzie, fast asleep, upstairs to her bedroom decorated with silver fairies, while Ben unloaded Mrs Maydew's microphone and music stand from the car. She placed Suzie on the bed, still dressed in her conger eel outfit. Isabel gently took a sticky bag of sweets from her hand. With a loud plonk, Rainbow the fairy fell through the window and collapsed on the bed by Suzie's feet.

'What kept you? You've been hours!' complained the fairy.

'The show ran late. The black dog isn't a werewolf,' whispered Isabel. The fairy raised her dark eyebrows. 'His real name's Wolven,' added Isabel.

Suzie snored and Rainbow jumped. 'Oh, she's your sister!' said Rainbow, peering at the sleeping Suzie, 'She's a scary child!' There was a clicking noise under the bed. 'What's that?' squeaked Rainbow.

'Oh no,' sighed Isabel. She lifted the corner of the bed cover. A large reddish brown lobster with spiky eyebrows looked up at her from the washing up bowl. 'I'll take you back to the Sea Life Park tomorrow,' Isabel promised. 'We've got some prawns in the freezer. I'll get you some in a minute.' Suzie stirred in her sleep, making 'munch, munch' noises.

'I'm leaving before she wakes up,' whispered Rainbow, perching on the window sill. There was a crash outside.

'Ow!' cried Ben from the garden path, staring up at Rainbow. He had dropped a speaker on his toe.

'I think he saw me!' said Rainbow.

Isabel laughed. 'Don't worry. He'll look you up in his *Moths and Butterflies of Portland* book and tell me he saw a very rare hawk-moth or something.'

'That's a relief,' said Rainbow. 'Goodbye, Isabel Maydew.' Rainbow leaped from the window and crashed into the bush by the kitchen door. She dusted herself off and disappeared into the night. Suzie opened one eye and smiled.

Isabel rested her elbows on the window sill. She looked out to sea. The moon threw a trickle of silver light across the sea towards the island. In the street outside her house, the pack of wolves stared up at her with unblinking golden eyes. The wolf cubs were batting each other playfully with their paws. The largest wolf with the thick snowy ruff across his chest crossed the street and stood below her home. Isabel smiled, glad to see the wolves again. They had shown her Wolven's past, his friend Stella Groves, and the snowy Isle from the end of the Ice Ages. For that, she thanked them. She had a feeling that one day she would meet the snow wolves again.

Suddenly the largest wolf turned and ran into the night, the rest of the pack following closely behind. A few flakes of snow trickled to the ground where the pack had rested. Over the deserted street, starlight flickered. Isabel looked wonderingly at the new constellation that stretched across the night sky where the Hunting Dog had sparkled for thousands of years.

To the east of Portland, as darkness turned the sea inky black, the mermaid swam with a tendril of seaweed wrapped around her arm as a bandage, turning Isabel Maydew over in her mind. She would be a fine prize, better than an enchanted dog or that annoying girl Miranda Greychurch. As the descendant of the island witch Agnes Maydew, the girl was shaping up well. The mermaid smirked. Isabel did not know she was using old island magic to time travel and explore the past. The mermaid decided to keep a closer eye on Isabel, as she swam south beneath the glittering stars.

In the peaceful darkness of Church Ope Cove, Wolven Groves sat alone on the mermaid's rock with his spear by his side and gazed up at the stars, dreaming of the future.

PHANTOM BLACK DOGS

I started my research for *Enchantment of the Black Dog* by walking around places on Portland associated with black dog stories. I tried to imagine what people had seen in the past and also what it might be like to meet a phantom black dog.

My first visit was to Cave Hole at Portland Bill, the lair of the menacing *Roy Dog*. A large shaggy black dog with one green and one red eye, he wears the freshly plucked eyes of his victims in his fur. In my story, Ben warns Isabel to beware the Roy Dog, as he often brings a warning of death and disaster. Skylark Durston, a famous Portland stone mason and poet, recounted a terrifying story about this dog. Retold in the 20th century, this story was probably first heard at least 100 or so years before. Two friends met the lighthouse keeper near Portland Bill one evening to go fishing. After fishing for a while, the friends left before the keeper and on the way home encountered the Roy Dog licking his paw. Worried about their friend, they returned to find the keeper lying dead with the claw of a huge dog on the end of his fishing line.

Another local Portland black dog is called the *Row Dog*, a ghostly animal with large saucer-shaped eyes, who wanders the paths of Portland at night. This dog blocks the walker's way, snarling and barking. I walked the paths that criss-cross the south of the Isle to try to work out who or what this creature may be. I wondered why he lurked on these paths and what message he was trying to give the people who meet him. As Isabel in my story is not easily scared, she faces this animal and asks him questions. She's braver than I am!

I looked at other black dogs in Dorset folklore. They are similar to the Row and Roy Dogs of Portland – large, shaggy, black dogs who appear and vanish suddenly. They are often associated with ancient footpaths or crossroads. Like the Roy Dog, they are also quite often found near water and during storms. And like the Row Dog, they are usually spotted at night.

Black dogs have a connection with mythology too. The black dog Anubis from ancient Egypt guided souls to the Underworld. The three-headed dog Cerberus in Greek and Roman myths guarded the gates of Hades (Hell). These stories left me wondering. Were phantom black dogs ever real? Or do they exist only in our imaginations? Black dogs certainly have a long and fascinating history.

During my research, I also looked at the four star dogs. If you study the stars during the spring, you will see the bright bluish-white *Dog Star* called *Sirius* low in the sky in the constellation called the *Great Dog*. Nearby is the *Little Dog* and higher in the skies are the *Hunting Dogs*, *Chara* and *Asterion*. These star dogs were created by ancient Greeks and Romans.

The black dog, friendly or frightening, raises a lot of questions. I've yet to see a spooky black hound myself. If you think you have or have any stories to tell about black dogs on Portland, please get in touch via my blog carolhunt. blogspot.com or Facebook page.

ABOUT THE AUTHOR

Carol is the author of *The Portland Chronicles*, a series of stories set on Portland. Her writing is inspired by the magic and mystery of the Isle and combines history with local myths and legends. She studied English Literature and History, has worked with young people as an adviser, and loves to share her writing experience and imagination with youngsters. Carol has three children and lives in Easton, Portland. In her free time, she tries to windsurf and enjoys walking, looking for sea dragons, fairies and spooky black dogs. Her blog (carolhunt.blogspot.com) and Facebook pages (Portland Chronicles and Portland Sea Dragon) have lots more interesting stuff about Portland and what she's up to, and she loves to hear from readers.

Carol sigining copies of her book *The Portland Sea Dragon* at the launch at White Stones Café with daughters Jade and Jasmine, mermaid and sea dragon.
(Photo courtesy of *View From Weymouth & Portland* free community newspapers, company name Lyme Media & Events Ltd.)

Have you read...

The Portland Sea Dragon?

first of THE PORTLAND CHRONICLES

'Adventures inspired by the sea .... Drawing on local history, *The Portland Chronicles* explore a seventeenth-century world of smuggling, witchcraft, piracy and intrigue.'

(*View From Weymouth and Portland*, 7 April 2010)

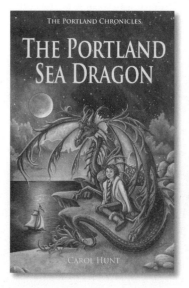

'*The Portland Sea Dragon* is an enchanting tale set in the near future. When the dragon is accused of the murder of Sally Lucke in 1616, only Isabel in 2011 can solve the mystery. So she sets out on a time-travelling adventure.'

(*The Free Portland News*, March 2010)

'There was standing room only at the launch of local author Carol Hunt's book, *The Portland Sea Dragon*, at White Stones Cafe in Easton on Portland as youngsters dressed as mermaids, sea dragons and pirates queued for their signed copy ... *The Portland Sea Dragon*, which is Carol's first book, is an all-Dorset production, with the book's artwork by Poole-based artist Domini Deane and published by husband and wife team Tim and Julie Musk of Dorchester-based *Roving Press.*'

(*Blackmore Vale Magazine*, 16 April 2010)

'A mum-of-three has achieved her dream of writing a children's book after being inspired by the legends of Portland ... *The Portland Sea Dragon* ... follows 12-year-old Isabel whose curiosity about the past draws her back to 1616 where she encounters an island witch and solves the mystery of a young woman's disappearance.'

(*Dorset Echo*, 27 February 2010)

'Heroes, villains and bedtime stories for all ... To assist the children with their story writing, they learnt about what it takes to be the hero or the villain, naughty or nice, good guy or bad guy. Special guest for the evening was author Carol Hunt who read extracts from her new book *The Portland Sea Dragon* ably assisted by two lovely puppets.'

(*View From Weymouth and Portland*, 17 March 2010)

About the Illustrator

Domini Deane is a self-taught artist, who has been creating magical worlds and creatures since she could pick up a crayon. Born in the Rocky Mountains of Colorado, she now lives and works in Dorset, England. Her favourite medium is watercolour with a pinch of fairy dust, and her greatest inspiration is a blank piece of paper. For more information visit www.dominideane.com.

'Young up-and-coming painter and illustrator Domini Deane paints fantastical watercolours and at 26 has just been published for the first time. Domini is like a Pre-Raphaelite  painting come to life, with her long auburn tresses and porcelain complexion – a perfect blend to complement her style of watercolour painting, which she has had an all-consuming passion for since she was old enough to hold a paintbrush.' (*Western Gazette*, 26 March 2010)

'Illustrator Domini Deane, whose artwork brings the mythical world to life, was also signing books and helping eager youngsters with their drawing' [at the launch of *The Portland Sea Dragon*]. (*View From Weymouth and Portland*, 7 April 2010).

'This was also the first book commission for Poole-based artist and illustrator Domini Deane, who provided the artwork for the book, capturing the mood and setting of the story in extraordinary detail.' (*thisisdorset.co.uk*, 14 April 2010)

OTHER ROVING PRESS TITLES